2.50

PIRACY
THESE CHARMING PEOPLE
THE GREEN HAT
THE ROMANTIC LADY
MAYFAIR
BABES IN THE WOOD
LILY CHRISTINE
MEN DISLIKE WOMEN
MAN'S MORTALITY
HELL! SAID THE DUCHESS
THE CROOKED CORONET

THE FIRST NOVEL LIBRARY

The London Venture

MICHAEL ARLEN

EDITED BY HERBERT VAN THAL

WITH AN

INTRODUCTION

BY

NOEL COWARD

CASSELL LONDON

CASSELL & COMPANY LTD
35 Red Lion Square, London WC1
Melbourne, Sydney, Toronto
Johannesburg, Auckland

First published by William Heinemann 1920. Copyright.
This edition © the estate of the late Michael Arlen 1968
New material © Cassell & Co. Ltd, 1968
This edition first published 1968

S.B.N. 304 92614 0

*Set in Monotype Garamond type and
printed in Great Britain by Cox & Wyman Ltd,
London, Reading and Fakenham*
F.368

WHAT is a novel? This pertinent question has been answered by a considerable number of critics, writers and novelists. One of our most admirable and eminent critics, Walter Allen, points out in his excellent survey *The English Novel*, 'Like any other artist the novelist is a maker. He is making an imitation of the life of man on earth.'

The novelist creates characters according to his view of life, and he creates a story around these characters, or a study —whether it is to inculcate right conduct, to reform manners, expose evils, social or otherwise—for an almost endless variety of purposes. He may set out merely to entertain, a thing many an admirable novelist has successfully done, winning multitudes of admirers. The novelist is also expected by his readers to be 'true to life', or he can, like Defoe, our first great novelist, benevolently hoodwink his public by declaring his narrative to be true. We often use the old cliché 'truth is stranger than fiction', but then we can assert with equal truth that fiction is often stranger than truth, and is none the worse for that. J. E. Baker has said,[1] 'The regular prose method is to put together a larger, more complex, more eccentric, or more subtle being out of the raw materials supplied by life. We recognize the creator's truth at every step, but the cumulative result exceeds anything within our ken.' The novelist may pursue his art as a most meticulous craftsman, and become one of the greatest influences on the modern novel, as did Henry James, or become an innovator of style and language as did James Joyce. The popularity of Dickens lay in his ability to create characters larger than life. On the other hand, as Somerset Maugham has said, 'A writer seldom writes as he would like to; he writes as he can: he is often aware of his defects; but he can rid himself of them as little as he can

[1] *History of the English Novel*, Vol. 1, p. 20.

change the colour of his eyes.' The present series encompasses every conceivable variety of the form, from the founder of the English novel to the day before yesterday. 'There is, however, a unique difference in this series in that every author is represented by his first work. Was that work indicative of what was to come? Could one forecast from his first novel his development or decline? The Introductions to the volumes written by experts, seek to answer these questions by giving the reader a survey of each chosen novelist by determining how his or her art evolved; what kind of a 'tree' resulted from those 'roots'? Those who became famous later in their careers and those whose total achievement brought them less fame are included in this Library of First Novels.

HERBERT VAN THAL

TO

THE SISTER

OF

SHELMERDENE

INTRODUCTION

by NOEL COWARD

IT is singularly appropriate that I should be asked to write an introductory preface to a re-issue of Michael Arlen's first book *The London Venture*, for it was the immediate success of this book that emboldened me, forty-three years ago, to ask Michael Arlen (Dikran) to lend me two hundred and fifty pounds to make up the capital for the production of my play *The Vortex* which was then in rehearsal at the Everyman Theatre, Hampstead. I telephoned him, guiltily conscious of my sordid motive, and he asked me to lunch at the Ritz. Early in the lunch, in fact during the potted shrimps, I blurted out my request and before I had time to explain to him why I needed the money, he had written out a cheque and handed it to me across the table. There were no provisos attached, no business-like arrangements for future 'interest' on the loan. He just gave it to me and went on recounting the plot of a short story he had in mind, a habit of his so strongly developed that it had become almost an addiction. I listened with only half my attention, being at the moment too preoccupied with my own feelings, which were gratitude, shame and an over-whelming relief. The reason I had been placed in this uncomfortable situation was that Mr Norman Macdermott, the managing director of the Everyman, had come to me a week before my play was scheduled to open and told me that unless two hundred and fifty pounds were immediately forthcoming the whole production would have to be abandoned. Owing to this generous gesture of Dikran's *The Vortex* opened the following week, was enthusiastically hailed by the critics and established me as the most promising playwright of the decade. Since that feverish and gratifying evening several decades have passed and I am happy to say that I still hold a tenuous right to that slightly ambiguous but, on the whole, optimistic appraisal. From then on Dikran's career and mine ran side by side for quite a while. The dramatized version of *The Green Hat* and *The Vortex* opened, equally triumphantly, on consecutive nights in New York in September 1925. It was rumoured, inevitably, that the two young writers were so consumed with jealousy of each other that they were not speaking. I was told by my hostess at a Park Avenue lunch party, that Michael Arlen was so envious of my success that he was barely able to contain his spleen. I replied that this was curiously obtuse of him as he happened to be one of the principal investors in it. After this Dikran and I decided that the time had come to scotch this nonsense and so, over a period of months, we solemnly had supper alone together once a week in the more fashionable New York night-clubs. The story was then spread that our relationship was, to put it delicately, out of the ordinary. We abandoned the struggle and, like Liberace, laughed merrily on our way to our separate banks.

On re-reading *The London Venture* I have been enchanted all over again with the unforced wittiness of Dikran's writing and the individual elegance of his style. His affectionate evocation of the various aspects of London in the early Twenties seems to me, a possibly prejudiced observer, to be remarkably undated. His descriptions of Bond Street, Soho, the walk from Hyde Park Corner to the Ritz, the charm of the Park itself on an afternoon of high summer are as delightful today as they were when he first wrote them. His use of the English language too, vivid, colloquial and only very rarely a trifle tentative, has surely never received the attention it deserves. Perhaps the blaze of his immediate commercial success blinded critical eyes to the fact that beneath the contemporary glitter of his prose and in spite of his fashionable acclaim, he was a writer not merely 'of promise' but of immediate and lasting achievement.

APOLOGIA PRO NOMINE MEO

OUT of consideration (in part) to such readers as may read this book I have assumed a name by which they may refer to me (if ever he or she may wish to do so kindly) in the same manner at least twice running—a feat of pronunciation which few of my English acquaintances have performed with my natal name. But there is also another reason, considerate of the author. I have been told that there are writers whose works would have been famous if only their names could have been familiarly pronounced—Polish and Russian writers for the most part, I gather. Since I had already taken every other precaution but this to deserve their more fortunate fate, in changing my name I have, I hope, robbed my readers of their last excuse for my obscurity.

DIKRAN KOUYOUMDJIAN.
'MICHAEL ARLEN.'

July, 1919.
SHEPHERD'S MARKET,
    MAYFAIR.

CHAPTER 1

MY watch has needed winding only twice since I left London, and already, as I sit here in the strange library of a strange house, whose only purpose in having a library seems to be to keep visitors like myself quiet and out of harm's way, I find myself looking back to those past months in which I was for ever complaining of the necessity that kept me in London. How I would deliver myself to a congenial friend about what men are pleased to call 'the artificial necessity of living'—a cocktail, that courtesan of drinks, lent some artificiality! With what sincerity I would agree with another's complaint of the 'monotonous routine of politeness,' without indulging which men cannot live decently; how I would mutter to myself of streets and theatres full of men and women and ugliness! Even as a cab hurried me through the Tottenham Court Road to Euston the smile which I turned to the never-ending windows of furniture shops was at the thought that I should not see them again for many days, and I could not imagine myself ever being pleased to come back to this world of plain women and bowler hats and bawdily coloured cinema posters, whose duty it is to attract and insult with the crude portrayal of the indecent passions of tiresome people. If there be a studio in purgatory for indiscreet aesthetics, Rhadamanthus could do no better than paper its walls with illustrations of 'The Blindness of Love,' or 'Is Love Lust?' For it is now a London of coloured drawings of men about to murder or be murdered, women about to be seduced or divorced. One has to see a crowd of people surging into a cinema, by whose doors is a poster showing a particularly vapid servant-girl, a harlot of the 'dark-eyed, sinister' type, and a drunken, fair-haired young man who has not yet realized that discretion is the better part of an indiscretion, before one can understand 'the lure of the screen.'

And even the entrance of Euston, rebuilt and newly painted, gave my eyes only the pleasure of foreseeing that the new

1

yellow paint would soon be dingy, and that the eyes of porters would soon no longer be offended with upstart colours which quarrelled with the greyness of their experience. And in the carriage I leant back and closed my eyes, and was glad that I was leaving London.

But the train had scarce left the station, and was whirling through the northern suburbs which should so fervently have confirmed my gladness, when I felt suddenly as though some little thing was being born inside me, as though some little speck of dust had come in through the open window, and fixed itself upon my pleasure at leaving London; and very soon I realized that this was the first grain of regret, and that I should not spend so many months away from London as my late depression had imagined. Then up will start the strong-minded man, and pish and pshaw me for not knowing my own mind. And if he does, how right he will be! For little do I care whether this mood be as the last, so they both fill up the present moment with fitting thoughts, and pain, and pleasure!

Now, I was already thinking of how I would return to London next year in the spring. What I would do then, the things I would write, the men I would talk to, and the women I would lunch with, so filled my mind, and pleasantly whirled my thoughts from this to that, that Rugby was long passed before even I had come to think of the pleasures that London in early summer has in store for all who care to take. When the days were growing long, it would be pleasant to take a table by the windows of the Savoy, and dine there with some woman with whom it would be no effort to talk or be silent.

Such a woman at once comes to my mind, with dark hair and grey-blue eyes, the corners of whose mouth I am continually watching because it is only there I find the meaning of her eyes, for she is a sphinx, and I do not yet know if what she hides is a secret or a sense of humour. You will say that that means nothing, and that she is quite invisible to you; but you do not know her, and I do—at least, I know that much of her. And with her it seems to me that I could dine only at that table by the windows where I could turn from her eyes to the slow-moving English river, and the specks of men and trams, which

2

are all that the leaves of trees will let me see of the Embankment. Perhaps I would tell her of that novel which I once began to write, but could never finish nor have any heart to try again, for it began just here at this table where we are now sitting; but the man was alone, and, if he ever lived outside my halting pages and had the finishing of my novel, he would put himself here again at the end, with you sitting in front of him. For that is the whole purpose of the novel, which I never realized till this moment, that once a young man was sitting here alone and wondering why that should be and what he should do, and in the end he was sitting here again with a woman for whom his passion had died, but whose eyes still made him talk so that he could not see the slow darkening of the river, or hear the emptying of the restaurant, until at last she laughed, and he had to stop because of the waiters who hovered round the table to relay it for the bored people who would come in from the theatres for supper. But all this I had never realized till I told you of it, and perhaps now I shall one day finish it, and call it 'Nadine,' for that is your name in the novel.

Thinking of the young man of my unfinished novel who had sat there so alone sent my thoughts back to the day not many years past when I first came to live in London. I am bitter about those first months, and will not easily forgive London for them; and if any young person shall begin to tell me how splendid were his first lonely days in the wilderness of people, how much he enjoyed the aimless wandering about the streets, how he liked to watch the faces of the people as they passed, laughing, or talking, or hungry, while he could do or be none of these for lack of company and convenience of means, then I will turn on him and curse him for a fool or a knave, and rend the affected conceit of his self-contained pleasure with my own experience and that of many others whom I know of. But then, for a young Englishman—how pleasant it is to write of 'young Englishmen,' as though one were really a foreigner!— the circumstances are a little different, and he need never taste that first absolute loneliness, which, as the weeks go by and the words are not spoken, seems to open out a vista of solitude

3

for all the days of life; nor need he be conscious that it is on himself—how, while it exaggerates, loneliness stifles self!—he must rely for every acquaintance, for every word spoken in his life. But for him there are aunts who live in Chester Square, and cousins who come up to stay a month or so at the Hyde Park Hotel, and uncles who live somewhere about Bruton Street, and have such a fund of *risqué* anecdotes that the length of Bond Street and Piccadilly will not see the end of them; and, perhaps, there are age-long friends of the family who have houses in Kensington and Hampstead, and 'nice' parquet floors on which you can dance to a gramophone; while for an Armenian, who soon realizes that his nationality is considered as something of a *faux pas*, there are none of these things, and he is entirely lost in the wilderness, for there is no solid background to his existence in another's country; and, as the days lengthen out and he grows tired of walking in the Green Park, he comes to wonder why his fathers ever left Hayastan; for it seems to me much better to be a murdered prince in Hayastan than a living vagabond in London. So I wandered about, moved my chambers gradually from Earl's Court to the heart of St James's, and read 'Manon Lescaut,' and sat in front of Gainsborough's 'Musidora' until I found that she had three legs, and could never look at it again.

Then, somehow, came acquaintance, first of the world, then of literature and its parasites; came teas at Golder's Green and Hampstead, and queerly serious discussions about subconsciousness; 'rags' at Chelsea, and 'dalliance with grubbiness,' and women. Through this early maze of ribaldry and discussion, the first of which bored me because of its self-consciousness, and because I do not like lying on the dirty floors of studios with candle grease dripping on me, and the latter which affected my years miserably and almost entirely perverted my natural amiability into a morbid distaste for living (which still breaks out at odd moments, and has branded me among many people as a depressing and damnably superior young person); through this maze of smoke and talk I can only still see the occasional personality of Mr D. H. Lawrence, as his clear, grey eyes—there is no equivalent to *spirituel* in

4

English—flashed from face to face, smiling sometimes, often but a vehicle for those bitter thoughts (and thoughts are so often conclusions with men af arrogant genius like Lawrence) which find such strange and emphatic expression in his books. I would need the pen of a De Quincey to describe my impression of that man, and I am candid enough to admit that I lack the ability, rather than the malice, which caused the little opium-eater to be so justly hated by such a man as Bob Southey. There is a bitterness which can find no expression, is inarticulate, and from that we turn away as from a very pitiful thing; and there is that bitterness which is as clear-cut as a diamond, shining with definitions, hardened with the use of a subtle reasoning which is impenetrable but penetrating, 'the outcome of a fecund imagination,' as Lawrence himself might describe it; a bitterness so concisely and philosophically articulate, that, under the guise of 'truth,' it will penetrate into the receptive mind, and leave there some indelible impressions of a strange and dominating mind. I have found that in the books and person of Mr D. H. Lawrence. He seems to lack humility definitely, as a man would lack bread to eat, and a note of arrogance, as splendid as it is shameless, runs through his written words; and the very words seem conscious that they are pearls flung before swine. He will pile them one on top of the other, as though to impregnate each with his own egotism, to describe the sexual passions of this man or that woman, words so full of *his* meaning, so pregnant with *his* passions, that at the end of such a page you feel that a much greater and more human Ruskin is hurling his dogmas at your teeth, that there is nothing you can say or think outside that pile of feeling which is massed before you, that you must accept and swallow without cavil and without chewing. With what relief one turns over a page and finds that here is no touch of flesh, but that Mr Lawrence is writing of earth! Let him sink into earth as deep as he may, he can find and show there more beauty and more truth than in all his arrogant and passionate fumblings in the mire of sex, in all his bitter striving after that, so to speak, sexual millennium, that ultimate psychology of the body and mind, which seems so to obsess him that in his writings he has buried his mind, as, in his own unpleasant phrase, a lover buried his head, in the 'terrible softness of a woman's belly.' Who has not read 'Sons and Lovers,' and laid it down as the work of a strange and great man, of the company of Coleridge, Stendhal, and Balzac? And who, as he read it, has not been shocked by a total lack of that sweetness which must alloy all strength to make it acceptable? 'That strange interfusion of strength and sweetness,' which Pater so admiringly found in Blake and Hugo, cannot be found in Mr D. H. Lawrence; there is a mass of passionate strength, that of an angry man straining with his nerves because he despises his hands; there is a gentleness in his writing of children which could never be capable of such melodrama as that in Mr Hardy's 'Jude the Obscure;' but in his men and women, in their day and night, there is no drop of sweetness. And I do not think he wishes it otherwise.

As the train flew through the Derbyshire countryside, whose brilliant sheen of the autumn sun, met the eye pleasantly with a rising and falling of pale yellowish green, with here and there a dark green patch of woodland, and made me want to stop the hurrying train and breathe the air of the place, my thoughts slipped back to the spring and the summer just before the war; and, with my eyes on the quickly passing sunshine on the low hills, I found that, after all, those last few months of peace had passed, perhaps, too lightly, too carelessly; but it was pleasant to think back to those days when lunches and dinners and weekends took up so much of one's time. I was glad now that I had not spent the three summer months in Yorkshire on the moors, where I should have been uncomfortable, and had to be for ever sending post cards to Hatchard's to post me this or that book, which would come when my mood for it had passed.

And how dreadful it is to want to read suddenly 'Love in the Valley,' and have to be content with Tennyson, to long for a chapter of Dostoieffsky, and be met with complete editions of Trollope and Surtees! So I see that my middle age will be crabbed and made solitary by my books, and that I shall never have the heart to leave them and go to the East to see the land

6

of my father Haik, or to walk about the lake upon which the great Queen Semiramis (who was the first in the world to discover that men could be conveniently changed into eunuchs) built the city Semiramakert, which is now called Van, and where later, when she was pursued by the swordsmen of her son, she threw a magic bracelet into the lake and turned herself into a rock, which still stands there covered with the triumphant script of the Assyrians.

CHAPTER 2

ONCE (in those far-off peaceful days when men still had enough grammatical sense to know that the word 'pacifist' does not exist, but that the less convenient 'pacificist' does) I had been very depressed for a week, and had scarcely spoken to anyone, but had just walked about in my rooms and on the Embankment, for I suddenly found myself without any money at all; and it is thus with me that when I am without money I am also without ideas, but when I have the first I do not necessarily have the last. I wondered if I had not done a very silly thing in being independent, and in not doing as my brothers had done, reading 'The Times' in an office every morning from ten to twelve, and playing dominoes in the afternoon, and auction bridge in the evening, and having several thousands a year when I was forty, and a Wolseley car to take my wife for a holiday to Windermere, because she looked pale, or because we were bored with each other. I smiled to think of the look on my brothers' faces if I suddenly appeared at their office one morning, and said that it was no good, and that I couldn't write, and was very hungry. I could not make up my mind whether they would laugh at me and turn me out, or whether they would teach me how to play auction and set me to answer letters about what had happened on such and such a day inst., and why the firm of —— thought it unnecessary that it should happen again, while they would sit in the next room, marked 'Private,' signing cheques and talking to visitors about the weather and the cotton markets. Perhaps I will do that some day, for, from what I have heard, it seems to me the easiest thing in the world to talk about rises and falls and margins without knowing anything about them at all.

The same thing happens with regard to books, for one often meets people who seem to have read every modern novel, and can discuss quite prettily whether Mr Wells is a man or a machine, or whether Mr Arnold Bennett, ever since he wrote the last lines to 'The Old Wives' Tales,' has not decided that it is better to be a merchant than a writer, or whether Mr E. V. Lucas thinks he is the second Charles Lamb, and what other grounds than his splendid edition has he for thinking so, or whether Mr George Moore does or does not think that indiscretion is the better part of literature, or whether Mr Chesterton or vegetarianism has had the greatest effect on Mr Shaw's religion; but then, after all this talk it turns out that they read 'The Times Literary Supplement' every week, and think Epictetus nothing to Mr Clutton-Brock, or they are steeped in Mr Clement Shorter's weekly criticism *en deshabille* in 'The Sphere.'

At last I could stand my depression no longer, and late one night, after a day in which I had spoken to no one but a little old woman who said that she wasn't a beggar but that God blessed the charitable, I sat down and wrote a long, conceited letter to Shelmerdene; for to her I can write whether I am gay or depressed, and be sure that she will not be impatient with me. I told her how I had a great fund of ambition, but had it not in me to satisfy a tenth part of it; for that is in the character of all my people; they promise much greater things in their youth than they can fulfil in their mature age. From twenty onwards they are continually growing stale, and bitter with their staleness; the little enthusiasm of their youth will not stretch through their whole life, but will flicker out shamefully with the conceit of their own precocity, and in trying to fly when other people are just learning to walk; and as the years pass on and youth becomes regret, the son of Haik, the faded offspring of a faded nation whose only call to exist is because it has lived so long and has memories of the sacking of Nineveh and Carchemish, is left without the impetus of development, with an ambition which is articulate only in bitterness; while the hardy Northerner, descendant of barbarian Druid worshippers whose nakedness was rumoured with horror in the courts and pleasure gardens of Hayastan and Persia, slowly grows in mind as in body, and soon outstrips the petty outbursts of the other's stationary genius. I told Shelmerdene that I, who had thought that England had given me at least some of her

9

continually growing enthusiasm, that *I*, who had thought I would not, like so many of my countrymen, be too soon stranded on 'the ultimate islands' of Oriental decay, was even now in the stage between the dying of enthusiasm and its realization; for the first impetus of my youthful conceits was vanishing, and there looked to be nothing left to them but an 'experience' and a 'lesson of life' without which I would have been much happier. In moods such as these one can hear in the far distance the wailing of a dirge, a knell, indefinitely yet distinctly, and the foreboding it brings is of an end to something which should have no end; a falling away, a premature decay which is like a growing cloud soon to cover the whole mind. . . . Shelmerdene, do you know the story of the Dân-nan-Rón, which Fiona Macleod tells? How there lived three brothers on the isle of Eilanmore: Marcus, who was 'the Eilanmore,' and Gloom, whose voice 'was low and clear, but cold as pale green water running under ice,' and Sheumais, on whose brow lay 'the dusk of the shadow.' Gloom was the wisest of the brothers, and played upon an oaten flute, which is called a *feadan*; and men were afraid of the cold, white notes of his barbaric runes, as he played his *feadan* from rock to rock and on the seashore; but most of all they feared the playing of the Dân-nan-Rón, which is the Song of the Seal and calls men to their death in the sea. And when the eldest brother, Marcus, was killed with the throwing of a knife, the murderer heard the words of Gloom, which said that he would hear the Dân-nan-Rón the night before he died, and lest he should doubt those words, he would hear it again in the very hour of his death. It happened as Gloom said: for one night the playing of the *feadan* drove the slayer, Manus MacCodrum, down into the sea, and as he battled madly in the water, and the blood gushed out of his body as the teeth of seals tore the life out of him, he heard from far away the cold, white notes of the Dân-nan-Rón.

This tale always bring to me that many men, in some sudden moment which even M. Maeterlinck would hesitate to define as 'a treasure of the humble,' hear the playing of a tune such as that, which tells them of some ending, unknown and indefinite, just as, in the moments of greatest love, a man will feel for a terrible second the shivering white ice of sanity, which tells him a different tale to that which he is murmuring to the woman in his arms. Men who have heard it must have become morose with the fear this distant dirge brought upon them; but of that foreboding nothing certain can be known, and it is only in such a mood as this, and to a Shelmerdene of women, that a fool will loosen his foolishness to inquire into such things. Clarence Mangan must have heard the tune as he lay drunk and wretched in his Dublin garret, for there is more than Celtic gloom in the dirge of his lines. John Davidson, whose poetry you so love, and who wrote in a moment of madness 'that Death has loaded dice,' must have heard it, perhaps when first he came to venture his genius in London, a young man with a strange, bad-tempered look in his eyes; and he must have heard the exulting notes, as clearly as did Manus MacCodrum, when he walked into the sea from Cornwall. Charles Meryon must have heard it as he walked hungrily about the streets of Paris, and wondered why those gargoyles —strange things to beautify!—on Notre Dame, into which he had put so much life, could not scream aloud to the people of Paris that a genius was dying among them for lack of food and praise. Do you remember, Shelmerdene, how you and I, when first I began to know you, stood before a little imp of wonderfully carved onyx stone which leered at us from the centre of your mantelpiece, and I said that it was like one of those gargoyles of Meryon's; and that afternoon I told you about his life and death, and when I had finished you said that I told the tale as though I enjoyed it, instead of being frightened by the tragedy of it? But I admired your imp of onyx stone very much, telling you that I loved its ravenous mouth and reptile claws, because they looked so helplessly lustful after something unattainable; and that same night I found a little black-and-gold box awaiting me in my rooms, in which was the imp of onyx stone, and a note saying that I must put it on my table because it would bring me luck. For a second I did not believe your words, but thought that you had given it to me to be a symbol for my helplessness, for I had said that it lusted after something utterly unattainable. But the second passed, and I found later that you had forgotten those words, and had sent it to me because I liked it. .... I would like to spend these glorious spring days away from London with you, in quietness, perhaps in Galway somewhere; but if you cannot come away with me tomorrow, I will take you out to dinner instead, and we will talk about yourself and the *ci-devants* who have loved you; and though I have no money at all now, I am quite sure that tomorrow will bring some.

Sure enough a few hours later I awoke to a bright spring morning, which brought happiness in itself, even without the help of a cheque which a recreant editor had at last thought fit to send me. As I walked out into the blaze of sunshine on the King's Road, I felt that I must surely be a miserable fellow to let my ill-nature so often oppress me that only very seldom I was allowed to enjoy such mornings as this; mornings which seem to spring suddenly out at you from a night of ordinary sleep, when, as you walk through streets which perhaps only the day before you hated bitterly, the spring sun wholly envelops your mind and comes between yourself and your petty dislikes, and the faces of men and women look brown, and red, and happy as the light and shadow play on them; such a day was this, a pearl dropped at my feet from the tiara of some Olympian goddess.

Later I telephoned to Shelmerdene to ask her to lunch with me instead of dine, as the day was so beautiful; but she said that she had already promised to lunch with someone, a man who had loved her faithfully for more than ten years, and as all he wanted from her was her company over lunch on this particular day of the week, she could not play him false, even though the day was so beautiful. But I told her that I would not be loving her faithfully for ten years, and that she must take the best of me while she could, and that on such a day as this it would be a shame to lunch with an inarticulate lover; for a man who had loved her faithfully for more than ten years, and wanted only her company over lunch once a week, must be inarticulate, or perhaps a knave whose subtle cunning her innocence had failed to unveil. So in the end we lunched together in Knightsbridge, and then walked slowly through the Park.

The first covering of spring lay on everything. The trees, so ashamed—or was it coyness?—were they of their bareness in face of all the greenness around them, were doing their best to hurry out that clothing of leaves which, in a few weeks' time, would baffle the rays of the sun which had helped their birth; and there was such a greenness and clearness in the air and on the grass, and about the flowers which seemed surprised at the new warmth of the world, hesitating as yet to show their full beauty; for they were afraid that the dark winter was playing them a trick and would suddenly lurch clumsily upon them again, that the Park has never seemed to me so beautiful as on that spring afternoon when a careless happiness lay about everything.

So far I have not said a word about Shelmerdene, except that she had found a man—or, rather, he had tiresomely found her—to love her faithfully for ten years, and she had so affected him that he thought a weekly lunch or dinner was the limit of his destiny with her. And yet, had he searched himself and raked out the least bit of gumption, he would have found he was tremendously wrong about her—for there were pinnacles to be reached with Shelmerdene unattainable within the material limits of a mere lunch or dinner. She was just such a delightful adventuress as only a well-bred mixture of American and English can sometimes make; such a subtle negation of the morals of Boston or Kensington that she would, in the searching light of the one or the other, have been acclaimed the shining light of their William Morris drawing-rooms. She drew men with a tentative, all-powerful little finger, and mocked them a little, but never so cruelly that they weren't, from the inarticulate beginning to the inevitable end, deliriously happy to be miserable about her. She was a Princess Casassimma without anarchical affectations; and like her she was almost too good to be true.

So much then, for Shelmerdene; for if to cap it all, I should go on to say that she was beautiful I would be held to have been an infatuated fool. Which, perhaps, I carelessly was, since I can't even now exactly fix upon the colour of her hair, doubting now in memory as I must have done actually on those past days with her, whether it was brown or black or, as sometimes on a sofa under a Liberty-shaded lamp, a silver-tinted blue, so wonderfully deep. . . . Perhaps destined, in that future when Shelmerdene is at last tired of playing at life, to be the 'blue silver' of the besotted madman to whom she, at the weary end, with but a look back at the long-passed procession of *ci-devants*, will thankfully give herself. *Dies iræ, dies illa.* . . .

CHAPTER 3

WE sat on chairs in the sun, and after we had been silent a long while, she began to do what women will never cease doing, so wise men say, as long as men say they love them, to define what the love of a man meant to a woman, and to explain the love of a man. She said that that man was wise who had said that love was like religion, and must be done well or not at all, but that she had never yet found in any man sincere love and delicacy, for there was always something coarse, some little note which jarred, some movement of the mind and body maladroit, in a man who is shown a woman's love. 'When men love and are not loved,' she said, 'often they keep their grace and pride, and women are proud to be loved by such men—even faithfully for more than ten years; but when men are loved and are confident, then they seem to lose delicacy, to think that love breaks down all barriers between man and woman; that love is a vase of iron, unbreakable, and not, as it is, a vase of the most delicate and brittle pottery, to be broken to pieces by the least touch of a careless hand. They seem to think that the state of love stands at the end of a great striving; they do not realize that it is only the beginning, and that the striving must never cease, for without striving there is no love, but only content. But they do not see that; they insist on spoiling love, breaking the vase with stupid, unconscious hands; and when it breaks they are surprised, and they say that love is a fickle thing and will stand no tests, and that women are the very devil. Always they spoil love; it comes and finds them helpless, puzzling whether to clothe themselves entirely in reserve or whether to be entirely naked in brutality; and generally they compromise, and, physically and mentally, walk about in their shirts.'

'As you say that,' I said, 'you remind me of that woman, Mrs Millamant, in Congreve's play, "The Way of the World." Do you remember that scene between her and Mirabell, when she attaches "provisos" to her consent to marry him? She says,

15

"We must be as strange as though we had been married a long time, and as well bred as though we had never been married at all." And it seems to me that she was right, and that you are right, Shelmerdene. Nowadays there is a reaction against convention, and such people make life unclean. They talk about being "natural," and succeed only in being boorish; they think that the opposite of "natural" is "artificial," but that is absurd, for why was the title "gentleman" invented if not for the man who could put a presentable glass on his primitive "natural" instincts in polite company? There must always be etiquette in life and in love, and there is no friendship or passion which can justify familiarity trying to break down the barriers which hide every man and every woman from the outside world. Men grow mentally limp with their careless way of living; and life is like walking on the Embankment at three o'clock in the morning, when London is very silent; and if you lounge along as your feet take you, your hands deep in your pockets, being "natural," you will see very little but the general darkness of the night and the patch of pavement on which your eyes are glued; but if you walk upright, your mind taut and rigid as it always must be except when asleep, then you will see many things; how the river looks strange beneath the stars, the mystery of Battersea Park which might, in the darkness, be an endless forest of distantly murmuring trees, the figure of a policeman by the bridge, a light here and there in the windows of the houses in Cheyne Walk, which might mean birth or death or nothing, but is food for your mind because you are living and interested in all living things. It was probably some wise philosopher, an Epicurean, and not a buffoon, as is supposed, who first uttered that saying which is now become farcical, that "distance lends enchantment." For he did not mean the material distance of yards and furlongs and miles, but the distance of necessary strangeness, of inevitable mystery, and of a rigid mental etiquette, the good manners of the mind. And that is why Henry James was a great man, and with a great propaganda. He was subtle with his propaganda —an ugly word which can be used for other things than the bawling of tiresome men in this Park on Sunday afternoons—

for he could do nothing without an almost obvious subtlety; but it is there in all his work, a teaching for all who care to be taught. In the world of Henry James—for he was more fastidious than Meredith or Mr Hardy and would have nothing to do with this world as it was, but made one of his own—in this world the men and women are not just men and women, with thoughts and doings bluntly and coarsely expressed as in real life; but he showed them to be subtle creatures, something higher than clever animals, with different shades of meaning in every word—what fool was it who said that a word spoken must be a word meant!—with barriers of reserve and strangeness between each person; and their conversation is not just a string of words, but a thing of different values, in which the mind of the speaker and the listener is alive and rigid to every current of refined thought which is often unexpressed but understood. I think "thin" is the right epithet for the minds of James' characters; and the difference between them and ordinary people is that within us there is a sort of sieve between the mind and the mouth, or in whatever way we choose to be articulate, which, unlike ordinary sieves, allows only the coarse grains to drop through and be given out, but keeps the subtleties and the refinement to itself; but between the minds and the articulation of James' people there are no sieves, and the inner subtleties and shades are given expression. There is a strangeness, a kind of mental tautness, a never-ceasing etiquette, about them all.'

But then I laughed, and when she asked me why I did not go on, I said that I had suddenly realized that I had strayed from the subject, and that whereas she had begun to talk of love I had ended by talking of Henry James. 'It is all about the same thing,' she said, 'for we are both grumbling at that mental limpness which makes people think that they need make no effort, but that life will go on around them just the same. And that is why I think one of the most dreadful sights is a man asleep. No one should see another person asleep; it seems to me the most private thing in the world, and if I were a man and a woman had watched me as I lay asleep, I should want to kill her so that she should not go about and tell people

17

how I had looked as I lay stupidly unconscious of everything around me. Only once I have seen a man asleep, and that was the end of a perfect love affair. I had suddenly gone to see him in his chambers, and when his man showed me into his room I found him lying there on the sofa, with his head thrown back on a cushion, sleeping. His man said that he must be very tired as he had been working all night, and that it would be kind of me not to wake him. I waited in the room for an hour, trying not to look at him but to read a book, but his breathing filled the room and I could not take my eyes away from him; and at the end of an hour I felt that my love had gone from me minute by minute as I had looked at him, and that now I might just as well get up and go away, for I did not care any longer if he was asleep or awake. So I went away, but I do not know if he woke up as the door closed behind me.'

'And did you ever tell him why you had ceased to love him?' I asked.

'I couldn't do that,' she said, 'because if he had not understood me I should have hated him, and I do not like hating people whom I have loved. But now I dine with him from time to time, and I can see that he is still wondering how it was that on Monday I loved him and on Tuesday I didn't.'

As we walked through the Park towards the Park Lane gates, it seemed to me wonderful that this day, one among many days, should already be passing, irrevocably, and that what we had said and what we had felt as we sat on chairs in the sun would never be repeated, would never come again except perhaps in a different way and with different surprises. And when I asked her if she felt the happiness of the afternoon, she laughed slightly and said that she liked the Park this spring afternoon. 'It is perfect now,' she said, 'but when we come here in a month's or two months' time it will be too warm to sit in the sun and talk about love and Henry James, and in the autumn we will sit down for a moment and shiver a little and pity the brown leaves falling, and in the winter we will walk quickly through because it will be too cold; and then in Park Lane you will put me into a taxi and stand by the door with your hat in your hand, and say good-bye. For the seasons will have gone round, and we shall each have given what the other will take, and when I look at you you will be different, and when you look at me you will not see, as you see now, my eyes looking far away over your shoulder, and you will not wonder what it is that I am looking at. For then, as you stand by the door of the taxi and smile your good-bye at me, the end will have come, and there will be nothing to look at in the distance over your shoulders. And next year you will be an "old friend," and I shall ring you up and say that I am very sorry I can't lunch and walk in the Park with you that day because an Oxfordish young man has fallen in love with me, and it will be amusing to see what sort of lunch he will order when he is in love.'

'But is a rose less beautiful because it is sure to die?' she said.

*   *   *

But the winter she spoke of was not of the seasons, for it rushed incontinently in upon us between the summer and the autumn, and, I too, was delicately added to the sedate statuary of Shelmerdene's 'old friends. . . .'

And now I am in this strange library whose rows of books stare so unfamiliarly at me. The table at which I write is by the big French windows, and I must be careful to keep my elbows from sprawling as they would, for everything is covered with dust, and if I were fussy and wiped it away I should raise a great cloud of it around my head. . . . All is quiet and leisurely this morning. Outside there is no sun or mildness to make me restless and self-conscious about my laziness; it is one of those days on which one need not think of doing anything which will be 'good for one,' and until about tea-time the outside world will be better to look at than to breathe. For the windows show me a very dark, wet-laden garden, and the steady rain falling among the last leaves of the trees and their myriad dead comrades on the grass and gravel makes that 'swish' which comes so coolly and pleasantly to ears which need not be wet with it. But at about five o'clock, if the rain has stopped by then, I shall go out and walk about the garden for an hour or so; I shall walk to the top of the Divvil Mound, which lies above half the county to the west and, on a fine day, gives your eyes a rugged length of the distant Cheviots, and there I shall look up to the sky and draw in long draughts of the fresh rain-scented air, and feel that I shall never be ill again in all my life; and as I walk back under the trees the wet will drip on to me and I shall splash myself here and there; but I shall not swear, for my clothes are done for the day, and when I get in I shall have a bath and change, and feel all new and clean for whatever the evening may bring.

Beside me now is an envelope with an American stamp, and that vaguely woe-begone look which readdressed envelopes have; for it followed me here some ten days ago from London, reaching me the same morning that I sat down to write this (for it has taken me more than a week of long mornings to write these few thousand words) which was at first to have been an essay on London, but seems now to have fallen into the state of a personal confession. Many times I have taken out this letter and re-read it, for it is a strange letter, such a one as a man may receive only once in his life. This letter needs no answer, for it is dead like the person who sent it; and that the sender should not now care if I read it or not gives me a queer feeling of triviality; for in her letter she asks me to write back, not knowing then that a letter from a dead person is the only sort one need not answer without blame or reproach.

The day has long passed when, if you felt inclined, you could moralize on death and the frailty of human life to your heart's content and be sure of a hearing. I am sorry that the common-places on death find now only impatient readers, for they make pleasant reading in the pioneer essayists from poor Overbury to Steele; for death, with all its embroideries and trappings of destiny and Nemesis, is a pretty way of exercising that philosophy which no one is without. I envy the courage of the man who could now write an essay 'On Death' as Bacon did once, laying down the law of it with no hint of an apology for the monotony of his subject; but there is now no essayist or philosopher with the calm and aloof assurance and arrogance of a Bacon, that you might see, after the last written words on the most trivial theme, this last seal, as though he were God, 'Thus thought Francis Bacon.' But of death there is nothing trivial and pleasant left to be said, and as a subject it has grown monotonous, except for the inevitable slayer and the slain, and that prevalent instinct for fair play ('the essential quality of the looker-on') which interests itself in the manner of the slaying.

But this letter has seemed strange to me because, perhaps, I shall never again receive a letter whose writer is dead, and who, when writing it, dreamt of all material things but death. Were I Oscar Wilde I might wonder now if English women who die in America come back to London; for there is much of London in the letter: 'I should like to be in London today —Bloomsbury London, Mayfair London, Chelsea London, London of the small restaurants and large draughts of wine, London of the intellectual half-lights, drone of flippant phrases and racy epigrams, with a thin fog outside; London of a resigned good humour, of modulated debauch moving like her traffic, strips of colour through dusk, and drab, optimistic, noisy solitude, tranquillity of incessant sound; autumn lamplight, busy park, sheep, men, women, prostitutes; doors slamming, people coming in and sitting by the fire, more cigarettes, cakes, shops, myriads of people. . . .'

But I would not like to be in London this month of November.

CHAPTER 4

BUT there was once a month of November, about which I could not so grandly say that I would not like to spend it in London; for something happened which threw me in a great hurly-burly of change into an uncomfortable little flat in Monday Road, which is in South Kensington; but for all the life and gaiety there is in it might just as well be in a scrubby corner of the Sahara on a dusty day. My father had died suddenly, and what little question there was of my ever going into business now dropped away, so I had to make at least a pretence of earning my living, or, rather, of making a career for myself. I was very definite about this, that I must *do something, be something*; for I had learnt this much of the world, that there is no room in it for casual comers, that a man must have a background (any background will do, but the more individual the better); that there is no room in any part soever of the social scale for a man who is just nothing at all; and as I have never seriously contemplated living exclusively in the company of landladies and their friends, I saw that I must put my back into it and cease being a very insignificant *rentier*. I couldn't bear the idea of going through life as just a complacent Armenian in a world where millions and millions of others were trying honestly and otherwise to climb up the greasy pole of respectable attainment.

But I cannot resist saying what I think of Monday Road, though I am sure I can do it no harm, because better men than I must have hated it, and more virulently. Monday Road, like all the other roads which sink their mutual differences into the so dreary Fulham Road, consists of large, equal-faced houses stuck together in two opposite rows which are separated by about fifteen yards or so of second-hand Tarmac; a road like another, you will mildly say, but you cannot possibly realize its dismal grimness if you have not lived there. The people who live in the angular-faced houses are artists who believe in art for art's sake—else they wouldn't be forced to live in the dismallest street in the world—amateur intellectuals like myself, and various sorts of women. The tribe of organ-grinders have a great weakness for Monday Road, probably because some tactless ass has stuck up a notice there that 'Barrel-organs are prohibited,' which is a silly thing to say if you can't enforce it. Altogether it is the sort of road in which a 'spinster lady' might at any moment lock her door, close her windows, turn on the gas, and read a novel to death. A woman in the flat next to mine did that a week after I arrived, and I have never viewed death more sympathetically.

When men grow old they are apt to discover pleasant memories attached even to the worst periods, as they thought them at the time, of their lives. I am not very old as yet, but looking back calmly on the eighteen months I spent in South Kensington, I can find here and there, through an exaggerated cloud of depression and wretchedness, a pleasant memory smiling reprovingly at me; as though, perhaps, I should not be treacherous to the good hours God or my luck had given me. . . . And there was one moment of them all, when, in the first darkness of an early autumn night, a dim, slight figure stood mysteriously on my doorstep, and I blinked childishly at it because I did not know who the figure was nor how it had come there—if indeed it had come at all, and I had not dreamed the ring of the bell which had startled me out of my book. Or, perhaps, she had made a mistake, hadn't come for me at all. . . .

But when she spoke, asking for me, I began to remember her, but only her voice, for I could not see her face which was hidden in the high fur collar of an evening cloak. She looked so mysterious that I didn't want to remember where I had seen her.

'I simply can't bear it,' she said nervously, 'if you don't remember me, I'll go away.' And she turned her head quickly to the gates where there stood the thick dark shape of a taxi which I had somehow not seen before, else I would have known for certain that she was not a fairy, a Lilith fairy, but just a woman; a nice woman who takes life at a venture. I decided, and said abruptly, 'Don't go.'

When we were upstairs in my sitting-room and I could see her by the light of eight candles, I remembered her perfectly well, though I had only seen her once before. We had met at some tiresome bridge party six months before, but just incidentally, and without enough interest on either side to carry the conversation beyond the tepid limits of our surroundings. And as I had never once thought of her since I had shaken myself free of them, I couldn't imagine how on earth she had known my address or even remembered my name, which she didn't dare try to pronounce, she had told me as we went up the stairs.

She said that she, too, had never thought about me at all since then, 'until tonight when I was playing bridge in the same room with the same people, except that you were not there—and I remembered you only suddenly, as something missing from the room. I didn't remember you because of anything you said, but because you had been the worst bridge player in the room, and had the most unscrupulous brown eyes that ever advised a flapper to inhale her cigarette smoke, as it was no use her smoking if she didn't. And thinking about you among those people who seemed more dreary than ever tonight, I had a silly homesick feeling about you as though we were comrades in distress, whereas I didn't even know your name properly and never shall if you don't somehow make it a presentable one.

'So I turned the conversation to Armenians in general, which is an easy thing to do, because you have only to murmur the word "massacre" and the connection is obvious, isn't it? Of course that sent that dear old snob, Mrs ——, off like mad, saying what bad luck it was for you being an Armenian, because you could so nicely have been anything else, and even a Montenegrin would have been a better thing to be; how surprised she had been when she met you, she told us, for she had always had a vague idea that Armenians were funny little old men with long hooked noses and greasy black hair, who hawked carpets about on their backs, and invariably cheated people, even Jews and Greeks ...

'But you are quite English and civilized really, aren't you?

24

I mean you don't think that, just because I managed to wangle out your address and came here on impulse, I want to stay with you or anything like that, do you?'

As she said that, I suddenly thought of Lord Dusiote's gallant villainy in Meredith's poem, and I told her quickly how a whole Court had been lovesick for a young princess, but Lord Dusiote had laughed, heart-free, and said:

> 'I prize her no more than a fling of the dice,
> But oh, shame to my manhood, a lady of ice,
>   We master her by craft!'

'But I seem to remember that my Lord Dusiote came to a bad end,' she laughed at me.

'Not so bad an end—it must have been worth it. And at least he died for a mistake, which is better than living on one:

> ' "All cloaked and masked, with naked blades,
>   That flashed of a judgment done,
> The lords of the Court, from the palace-door,
>   Came issuing forth, bearers four,
>   And flat on their shoulders one." '

But Lord Dusiote's gallant death left her quite cold, for she was suddenly by the bookcase, running caressing fingers over a binding here and there.

'What perfectly divine books you have! I shall read them all, and give up Ethel M. Dell for good—but you are probably one of those stuffy people who "take care" of their books and never lend them to any one because they are first editions or some such rubbish.'

'You can have them all,' I said, 'and you can turn up the corner of every page if you like, and you can spill tea on every cover or you can use them as table props, because all these books from Chaucer to Pater are absolute nonsense at this moment, for in not one of them is there anything about a dark-haired young woman with blue eyes and a tentative mouth, and the indolent caress of a Latin ancestress somewhere in her voice, standing on a doorstep in a dingy road, calling on a man who might quite easily be a murderer, for all you know.'

25

But enough of that, for the situation of a young man and a young woman in a third-floor flat miles away from anywhere that mattered, at eleven o'clock on such a warm autumn night as makes all things seem unreal and beautiful, is a situation with a beard on it, so to speak.

When I first knew Phyllis, though always candid, she was inclined to be rather 'county,' the sort of woman 'whose people are all service people, you know;' she lived with her mother, near Chester Square, who at first disliked me because I was not in the Brigade of Guards, but later grew quite pleasantly used to me since I, unlike the Brigade of Guards, it seems, did at least acknowledge my habitual presence in her house by emptying Solomon's glory into her flower vases; and if there's a better reason than gratitude for getting into debt, tell it to me, please.

But Phyllis, like many another good woman of these Liberal times, turned her bored back on 'county,' and only remembered what was 'done' the better not to do it; fought for, and won a latchkey; asserted her right to come home at night as late as she pleased, and *how* she pleased—for she had come home from a dance one night on a benevolent motor-lorry, which she had begged to pick her up on Piccadilly in pity for her 'tired bones,' and which, incumbrously dropping her at mother's door, woke up the whole street. And I can so well imagine Phyllis, as she fitted in her latchkey, murmuring languidly, but without much conviction, 'What fun women have . . .'

But, in the reaction of her type against the preceding age of Victoria, she went to the other extreme; saw life too much through the medium of a couple of absinthe cocktails before each meal and sex too much as though it were entirely a joke, which it isn't . . . quite. She cut her hair short, and took to saying 'damn' more often than was strictly necessary. In fact, she would have been quite unbearable if she hadn't been pretty, which she delightfully was. And, unlike her more careless sisters of Chelsea, Hampstead, and Golder's Green, she did not make the terrible mistake of dressing all anyhow, or make a point of being able to 'put up with anything;' such as, sleeping

26

on studio floors after a party, in such a way as to collect the maximum amount of candle grease and spilled drink on her skirts, and wearing men's discarded felt hats, cut as no decent man would be seen alive wearing one, and Roger Fry sort of blouses which don't quite make two ends meet at the back, and carrying queer handbags made, perhaps, out of the sole of a Red Indians' threadbare moccasin ... Bohemians indeed, but without so much as a 'Bo' anywhere about them!

They can 'stand anything,' as they have let it be generally known. But, by dressing like freaks and by being able to stand anything, they have detracted considerably from their attraction for men; for freaks are well enough in freakland but look rather silly in the world as it is—which is the world that matters, after all; and what the devil is the good of being polite and making a fuss of a woman if she tells you repeatedly that she can 'stand anything,' and much prefers the feeling of independence fostered by lighting cigarettes with her own matches, and opening doors with her own so unmanicured fingers?

I suddenly realize at this very moment of writing why those months in South Kensington seemed so overpoweringly dismal, and that even now it is only time which lends a real pleasure to the memory of the tall, dim figure (Mr Charles Garvice would have called her 'sylph-like.' I wish I were Mr Garvice) which stood on my doorstep on an autumn night, and so mysteriously asked for me. For that beginning had a dreary end, as indeed all endings are dreary if the silken cord is not swiftly and sharply cut, thus leaving a neat and wonderful surprise, instead of the long-drawn ending of frayed edges and worn-out emotions which drive quite nice young men into a premature cynicism of dotage.

For we very soon tired of each other, and began to slip away into our different lives with a great deal of talk about our 'wonderful friendship;' though we both of us knew very well that there is nothing left to eat in an empty oyster, and nothing to talk about on a desert island except how deserted it is, and nothing to look forward to when you have too quickly reached *Ultima Thule* but to get as quickly back again and examine

27

your bruises—but he is a coward who hasn't enough kick left in him to begin again and repeat his mistake, for though two wrongs may not make a right, three or four mistakes of this sort do certainly make a man. . . . So we both set out to get back again, but not as quickly as possible, because Phyllis is a woman, and, perhaps, I am by way of having a few manners left—and, therefore, we had to take the longest way back; and were both very tired and bored with each other when at last I suddenly left her one night after dinner at her house at half-past nine, because I had a headache—'my dear, aspirin isn't any good, really it isn't'—and was sure she had one, too . . .

Six months ago I had a letter from her, saying that she was going to marry a nice fat baronet, a real, not a Brummagem one, and not so much because of his money, but because of his nice, solid, middle-class ideas, which would help to tone down hers. Phyllis was like that, and I've often wondered very much about that wretched baronet, whether he will tone her down, or whether she will persuade him to open a hat shop off Bond Street in aid of a 'bus conductors' ' orphanage.

Phyllis, Phyllis, you really can't go through life with half a cold grouse in one hand and a pint of Cliquot '04 in the other. There are other things . . . so they say.

CHAPTER 5

Iт shames me a little to confess that I have always fitted in my friends to suit my moods; for it may seem superior of me, as though I attached as much importance to my moods as to my friends, and therefore too much to the former; but it is really quite natural and human, for there is no man, be he ever so strong, who does not somehow sway to his moment's mood as a great liner imperceptibly sways to the lulling roll of the seas, as compared to myself, a rickety, rakish-looking little craft which goes up to the skies and down into the trough to the great swing of those mocking waves—moods!

But I, as I say, unlike that strong man who will pretend to crush his mood as some trifling temptation to relax his hold on life, I am so sociable a person that I must give my friends every side of myself and to each friend his particular side. And, though I do not wish to seem superior I have so far mastered the art of friendship, of which Whistler made such a grievous mess, that that side of me which such and such a friend may like is the side which I happen to wish to show to him. I keep it for him, labelling it his; when I see him in the distance I say, 'Dikran, up and away and be at him;' for I think it incumbent on people who, like myself, are not really significant, to be at least significant in their relations with others, to stand out as something, even as a buffoon, among their acquaintances, and not be just part of the ruck. My ideal is, of course, that splendid person of Henry James', in 'The Private Life,' who faded away, did not exist, when he was alone, but was wonderfully and variably present when even a chambermaid was watching him. That subtle, ironic creation of Henry James' is the very incarnation of a Divine Sociability, but in actual life there is no artist perfect enough to give himself so wholly to others that he literally does not exist to himself.

I am not selfish, then, with my moods; with a little revision and polishing I can make them presentable enough to give to my friends as, to say vulgarly, the real article, the real me. And of them all there is one special mood, a neutral-tinted, tired, sceptical thing, which I have come to reserve exclusively for my friend Nikolay, who lives in a studio in Fitzroy Street, and faintly despises people for living anywhere else.

When I had pressed his bell I had to step back and watch for his face at the third-floor window, which, having emerged and grunted at me below, would dwindle into a hand from which would drop the latchkey into my upturned hat. Then very wearily—I had to live up to my mood, you see, else why visit Nikolay?—I would climb the stone steps to his studio.

Once there, I resigned myself to a delicious and conscious indolence. My thoughts drifted up with my cigarette smoke, and faded with it. My special place was on the divan in the corner of the large room, under a long shelf of neatly arranged first editions, from which I would now and again pick one, finger it lazily, mutter just audibly that I had bought that same book half-a-crown cheaper, and relapse into silence. If uncongenial visitors dropped in, I would abuse Nikolay's hospitality by at once turning over on my left side and going to sleep until they had gone. But generally no one came, and we were alone and silent.

From the divan I would watch Nikolay at work at his long table in front of the window, through which could be seen all the chimneys in Fitzroy Street, Charlotte Street, and Tottenham Court Road. How he could do any work at all (and work of colour!) with the drab cosmopolitanism of this view ever before his eyes, I do not know; myself would have to be very drunk before I could ignore those uncongenial backs of houses and chimneys, stuck up in the air like the grimy paws of a gutter-brat humanity. For an hour on end, until he turned to me and said, 'Tea, Dikran?' I would watch him through my smoke, as though fascinated by the bent, slight figure as it drew and painted, with so delicate a precision of movements, those unreal and intangible illustrations, which tried at first to impress one by their drawing or colouring, but seemed to me mainly expressions of the artist's grim and ironic detachment from other men; a *macabre* observer, as it were, of their passions, himself passionless, but widely, almost wickedly, tolerant. An erect satyr in topsy-turvydom.

If it were any other man than Nikolay, I would know him well, for I have seen much of him; but one knows men by their 'points of view,' and I am not sure that Nikolay ever had one. He was, or rather he seemed definitely to be, curiously wise; one never put his wisdom to the test; one never heard him say an overpoweringly wise thing, but there was no doubt that he was wise. People said he was wise. Women said it. A strange man, indeed; queer, and a little sinister. Perhaps six hundred years ago he might have been an alchemist living in a three-storied house in Prague, exiled from his native land of Russia for criticizing too openly the size of the Czarina's ears; for Nikolay knows no fear, he can be ruder than any man I know. I have heard him answer a woman that her new hat didn't suit her at all. 'I think it is a rotten hat,' he said, and the vanity of an admitted thirty years faded from her, and she was as a dejected *houri* before the repelling eyes of a Salhadine.

He had not always been so detached and passionless. Steps of folly must somehow have led up to that philosophic wisdom which so definitely obtruded on the consciousness; so definitely, indeed, that I have watched women, as we perhaps sat round the card-table in his studio, and seen them in their manner defer to him, as though he were a great man in the eyes of the world, which he isn't. But to be treated as a great man, even by women, when you are not a great man, is indeed the essence of greatness! Bravo, Nikolay! I see you, not as I have always seen you, but in Paris, where rumour tells of you; in Paris, where your art was your hobby and life your serious business, and a dress suit the essential of your visibility of an evening.

I feel riot and revelry somewhere in you, Nikolay; the dim green lights of past experiences do very queerly mock the wisdom in your contemplative eye. I am to suppose, then, that you have seen other things than the rehearsals of a ballet, have marvelled at other things than the architecture of Spanish-Gothic cathedrals? Ah, I have the secret of you! You are a medieval, a knight of old exotic times, a Sir Lancelot without

31

naïveté. Now, as the years take you, it is only in your drawings that your mind runs cynically riot among the indiscretions of literature—what a sinister inner gleam I espied in you when you told me that you were going to illustrate the poems of François Villon! But in Paris, long ago, I see you, Nikolay, standing in the curtained doorway of a cushion-spread studio, where the lights shine faintly through the red arabesques patterned on the black lamp shades. I see you standing there with a half-empty glass of Courvoisier in your hand, sipping, and watching, and smiling . . . And women, perhaps—nay! a princess for very certain, it is said—running wild over the immobility of your face, immobile even through those first perfervid years.

But it did not always happen that I found him working at his table by the window. Sometimes he would be pacing restlessly up and down the room, and round the card-table in the centre (which was also a lunch, tea, and dinner-table).

'I have never before been four years in one place,' he said. 'I have never been six months in one place.' He related it as a possibly interesting fact, not as a cavil against circumstances. It shows what little I knew of, or about, him that I had never before heard of his travels.

'But how have you ever done any work if you never stayed in one place, never settled down?'

'Settled down!' He stopped in his walk and fixed on me with a disapproving eye. 'That's a nasty bad word, Dikran. The being-at-home feeling is a sedative to all art and progress. In the end it kills imagination. It is a soporific, a—what you call it?—a dope. There's a feeling of contentment in being at home, and you can't squeeze any creation out of contentment.

'Permanent homes,' he said, 'were invented because men wanted safety. The safety of expectation! Imagination is a curse to most men; they are not comfortable with it; they think it is unsettling. Life is an experiment until you have a home, and feel that it is a home. Men like that. They like the idea of having a definite pillow on which to lay their heads every night, of having a definite woman, called a wife, beside them. . . . Bah! Charity begins at home, and inertia stays there. Safety doesn't

breed art or progress—and when it does, it miscarries—the
Royal Academy . . .

'Men want homes,' he said, 'because they want wives. And
they generally want wives because they don't want to be
worried by the sex-feeling any more. They don't want women
left to their own imagination any more. They want the thing
over and done with for ever and ever. Safety! Men are not
adventurous. . . .'

He turned to me sharply. 'Look at you!' he said. 'Have you
done anything? Since I have known you, you have done
nothing but write self-conscious essays which "The New Age"
tolerates; you have played about with life as you have with
literature, as though it were all a question of commas and
semi-colons. . . . You have tried to idealize love-affairs into a
pretty phrase, and in your spare time you lie on that divan and
look up at the ceiling and dream of the luxurious vices of
Heliogabalus. . . . You are horribly lazy, not adventurous at
all. What's it matter if your cuffs get dirty as long as your hands
get hold of something?'

'One can always change one's shirt, if that is what you
suggest, Nikolay. But you are wrong about my not being
adventurous—I shall adventure many things. But not
sensationally, you know. I mean, I can't look at myself straight,
I can only look at myself sideways; and that perhaps is just as
well for I overlook many things in myself which it is good to
overlook, and I can smile at things which James Joyce would
write a book about. And when I write a novel—for of course
I will write one, since England expects every young man to
write a novel—the quality I shall desire in it will be, well,
fastidiousness. . . . I come from the East; I shall go to the
East; I shall try to strike the literary mean between the East
and the West in me—between my Eastern mind and Western
understanding. It will be a great adventure.'

'The East is a shambles,' he said shortly. And in that
sentence lay my own condemnation of my real self; if any hope
of fame ever lay in me, I suddenly realized it was in that acquired self which had been to a public school and thought it
not well bred to have too aggressive a point of view. Oh, but

33

what nonsense it all was! I lazily thought—this striving after fame and notoriety in a despairing world ...

I looked at Nikolay, who had done all the talking he would do that day, and was now sitting in an arm-chair and staring thoughtfully at the floor; thoughtfully, I say, but perhaps it was vacantly, for his face was a mask, as weird, in its way, as those fiendish masks which he delighted in making. And, as I watched him like this, I would say to myself that, if I watched long enough, I would be sure to surprise something; but I never surprised anything at all, for he would surprise me looking at him, and his sudden genial smile would bring him back into the world of men, leaving me nothing but the skeleton of a guilty and ludicrous fancy; and of my many ludicrous fancies about my friend this was indeed the most ludicrous, for I had caught myself thinking that he was not really a man at all, but just part of a drawing by Félicien Rops ...

CHAPTER 6

From my flat in Monday Road to Piccadilly Circus was a long way, and the first part of it wearisome enough through the Fulham Road, with its cancer and consumption hospitals, its out-of-the-centre dinginess, its thrifty, eager-looking, dowdy women, and its decrepit intellectuals slouching along with their heads twisted over their shoulders looking back for a bus, on the top of which they will sit with an air of grieved and bitter dislike of the people near them. But at Hyde Park Corner I would get off the bus, for I have a conventional fondness for Piccadilly, and like to walk the length of it to the Circus.

I like to walk on the Green Park side; in summer because of the fresh, green, rustling trees, an unhurried pleasaunce in London's chaotic noises, and in winter because I like nothing better than to look at leaf-stripped trees standing nakedly against a grey sky, finger-posts of Nature pointing to the real No-Man's Land, and illustrating the miraculous wonder of being just beautiful, as no man-made thing can be; for all things made by man, a picture, or, if you like, a woman's shoes with heels of stained majolica, have an aim and a purpose. They lack the futility, of which Nature alone has the secret, of being just carelessly beautiful. When I say Nature, I do not see the Dame Nature of Oscar Wilde's crooked vision, a crude, slatternly char-woman, but a spendthrift prodigal, spending for the sheer love of spending; he takes every man by the sleeve, and with delicious good manners he makes it seem that he values your opinion above all others, that he has created the beauty of the world to please in particular your eye, that you will sadly disappoint him if you hint that you hadn't much liked the tinge of vermilion in yestereen's sunset, for he had touched in that vermilion just to give you a pleasant surprise.

Thus it is with Nature and myself; I see him as an old beau, given to leering in cities, but frank and natural in open places.

35

And he knows me well, too; knows I am no minor poet, no poet at all, in fact, and, therefore, not to be gulled by insincere sunsets and valleys without shade or colour; that the idea of a fawn skipping about where I don't expect him, far from causing in me a metrical paroxysm after Mr Robert Nichols, frankly bores me; he has shown me an odd nymph here and there, but I haven't encouraged him. ... They are so intangible, I thought, and they faded away. So at last, in desperation, he stuck up a naked tree against a grey sky, and I thought it beautiful. It is a matter entirely between the old beau and myself. For all I care, you may think my stripped tree a stupid old tree, but to me it is beautiful. I see life that way.

But the day I am thinking of, when I got off the bus at Hyde Park Corner, was towards the end of October, when oysters have already become a commonplace; and as I walked up the Green Park side, the path around me was strewn with brown and red and faded green leaves, the last sacrifice of autumn to winter. I wondered why all things did not die as beautifully and as naturally as autumn dies. If all things died like that, there would be no fear in the world, and a world without fear would be just a splendid adventure, and life would be like chasing a sunset to the Antipodes—it would disappear only to appear again, more wonderfully.

But the fear of the shapeless bogey behind existence has been the peculiar gift of God; for so long He has chosen to be secretive about death, and the secret of it is in the eating of the last remaining apple on the Tree of Knowledge. But, O God, it is all a vain secrecy, this about death. Man was not made to be so easily satisfied. Education may have made him ignorant, but he was born inquisitive. Some day, some day, a more subtle and less solid Conan Doyle will arise, and valiantly catch a too indiscreet ancestral ghost, and holloa to a professor to X-ray his astral vitals, to find out by what means and processes came a living man to be a dead man and then an ancestral ghost. Their discoveries will then be written down in the form of a memoir and made into a fat book, complete with a spiritual preface and an astral index, and will cause a great stir in the world. But it will be a great shame on the Tree of Knowledge to have its last apple knocked down from it by a paltry book.

This last week or so of autumn is the time of all times when the fanatic hermit, sitting alone in his desert place, should be tolerant of the world's frailty. If such an one would let me, a worldly enough young man, approach him, I would tell him of the great joy there is in walking with a loved woman on crisp wind blown leaves, under country trees, with tea soon to be ready before a big fire in the house half a mile away. At that my hermit would look at me angrily, for a fleshly young man indeed; but I would go on to tell him of how there is no splendour anywhere like to the splendour of a youth's dreams at that quiet time; dreams that may be of a palace made of dead leaves, with terraced pleasure gardens fashioned out of autumn air, in which he would walk with his mistress, and be a king and she a queen of more than one world. . . .

As though for the first time, I noticed that afternoon a sheen of livid copper over the scattered leaves, and I said to myself that it was an undefinable addition to their beauty, like the sheen of blue in the dark hair of Shelmerdene, as she sat in the corner of a sofa under a Liberty-shaded lamp.

The passing thought of Shelmerdene fixed my attention through the Park railings on the prostrate figures here and there of men sleeping, for it was a very mild afternoon for late October. Sleep was her foible, the hobby-horse on which she would capriciously ride to heights of unreason whither no man could follow her and remain sane. She admitted that she herself had, occasionally, to sleep; but she apologized for it, resented the necessity. And, as I walked, I saw a sleeping, dejected figure too near the Park railings as though with her eyes, and was as disgusted. But I smiled at the memory of her wild flights of mythical reasoning.

'The mistake Jehovah made,' I heard her saying, 'was to teach Adam and Eve that it was pleasanter and more comfortable to lie and sleep on the same well-worn spot in Eden every night than to move about the Garden and venture new resting places. It was a great mistake, for it gave sleep a definite and important value, it became something to be sought for in a special and comfortable place. Sleep ceased to be a careless lapse, as it had been at first when Adam madly chased the shadow of Lilith through the twilight. In the company of Eve sleep was no more a state for the tired body, and only for the body, but it became a thing of the senses; so many hours definitely and defiantly flung as a sop to Time. Sleep became part of the business of life, whereas, in those first careless days of Adam's unending pursuit of Lilith, it had been only part of the hazard of life.

'If Lilith had been allowed to have the handling of Adam,' she said, 'instead of Eve, who was the comfortable sort of woman "born to be a mother," sleep, as we know it, would never have happened; unnecessary, gluttonous sleep, the mind-sleep!

'Lilith was a real woman, and very beautiful. She was the first and greatest and most mysterious of all courtesans—as, indeed, the devil's mistress would have to be, or lose her job. She must have had the eyes of a Phœnix, veiled and secret, but their secret was only the secret of love and danger—Danger! Jehovah never had a chance against Lucifer, who was, after all, a man of the world, in his fight for the soul of Lilith. She never had a soul, and it was of Lilith Swinburne must have been thinking when he wrote "Faustine," which silly fools of men have addressed to me. ... Of course, she chose Lucifer. Who wouldn't choose a dashing young rebel, a splendid failure if ever there was one, with a name like Lucifer, as compared to a darling, respectable, anxious old man called Jehovah? It's like asking a young woman to choose between Byron and Tolstoi . . .'

But Shelmerdene had long since gone, to play at life and make fools of men; to make men, to break men, they said of her, and leave them in the dust, grovelling arabesques on the carpet of their humiliated love. 'Let them be, let them be in peace,' I had said to her impatiently, but she had turned large, inquiring, serious eyes on me, and answered, 'I want to find out.' She had, indeed, gone 'to find out'—to Persia, they said, on a splendid, despairing chase. And I saw a vision of her there, but not as the proud, beautiful creature who filled and emptied a man's life as though for a caprice; I saw her on her knees in a ruined pagan temple on a deserted river bank, purified, and satisfied, and tired, entreating the spectre of the monstrous goddess, Ishtar, to let her cease from the quest of love ... I am so tired, she is saying to the nebulous goddess who has fashioned the years of her life into a love-tale. But who is Shelmerdene to beg a favour from Ishtar, who, in the guise of Astarte in Syria and Astaroth in Canaan, upset the gods and households of great peoples and debauched their minds, so that in later ages they were fit for nothing but to be conquered and to serve Rome and Byzantium as concubines and eunuchs?

Poor, weak Shelmerdene! Slave of Ishtar! Didn't you know, when, as a young girl, you set yourself, mischievously but seriously, 'to find out' about men and life, that you would never be able to stop, that you would go on and on, even from Mayfair to Chorasan? You should have known. You have been so wantonly blind, Shelmerdene. You have idealized tomorrow and forgotten today—and now, perhaps, you are on your knees in a ruined temple in the East, begging favours of Ishtar. Not she to grant you a favour! Trouble has always come to the world from such as she, a malignant goddess. It has been said that Semiramis conquered the world, and Ishtar set it on fire. . . .

CHAPTER 7

I ASKED her once, but long after I had realized that loving Shelmerdene could not be my one business in life, if she did not feel that perhaps—I was tentative—she would some day be punished. 'But how young you are!' she said. 'You don't really think I am a sort of Zuleika Dobson, do you?—just because one wretched man once thought it worth while to shoot himself because of me, and just because men have that peculiar form of Sadism which makes them torture themselves through their love, when they have ceased to be loved. . . . It's a horrible sight, my dear—men grovelling in their unreturned emotions so as to get the last twinge of pain out of their humiliation. I've seen them grovelling, and they knew all the time that it would do no good, merely put them farther away from me—or from any woman, for the matter of that. But they like grovelling, these six-foot, stolid men.'

'But haven't *you* ever been on your knees, Shelmerdene?'

'Of course I have. Lots of times. I always begin like that—in fact, I've never had an affair which didn't begin with my being down and under. I am so frightfully impressionable. . . .

'You see,' she touched my arm, 'I am rather a quick person. I mean I fall in love, or whatever you call my sort of emotion, quickly. While the man is just beginning to think that I've got rather nice eyes, and that I'm perhaps more amusing than the damfool women he's known so far, I'm frantically in love. I do all my grovelling then. And, Dikran! if you could only see me, if you could only be invisible and see me loving a man more than he loves me—you simply wouldn't know me. And I make love awfully well, in my quiet sort of way, much better than any man—and different love-speeches to every different man, too! I say the divinest things to them—and quite seriously, thank God! The day I can't fall in love with a man seriously, and tell him he's the only man I've ever *really* loved, and *really* believe it when I'm saying it—the day I can't do that I shall know I'm an old, old woman, too old to live any more.'

'Then, of course, you will die?' I suggested.

'Of course I will die,' she said. 'But not vulgarly—I mean I won't make a point of it, and feel a fat coroner's eyes on my body as my soul goes up to Gabriel. I shall die in my bed, of a broken heart. My heart will break when I begin to fade. I shall die before I have faded. . . .'

'No, you won't, Shelmerdene,' I said. 'Many women have sworn that, from Theodosia to La Pompadour, but they have not died of broken hearts because they never realized when they began to fade, and no man ever dared tell them, not even a Roi Soleil.'

'Oh, don't be pedantic, Dikran, and don't worry me about what other women will or won't do. You will be quoting the "Dolly Dialogues" at me next, and saying "Women will be women all the world over."'

'It is always like that about me and men,' she said. 'I burn and burn and fizzle out. And all the time the man is wondering if I am playing with him or not, if it is worth his while to fall in love with me or not—poor pathos, as if he could help it in the end! And then, at last, when he realizes that he is in love, he begins to say the things I had longed for him to say four weeks before; every Englishmen in love is simply bound to say, at one time or another, that he would adore to lie with his beloved in a gondola in Venice, looking at the stars; any Englishman who doesn't say that when he is in love is a suspicious character, and it will probably turn out that he talks French perfectly.

'And when at last he has fallen in love,' she said dreamily, 'he wants me to run away with him, and he is very hurt and surprised when I refuse, and pathetically says something "about my having led him to expect that I loved him to death, and would do anything for or with him." The poor little man doesn't know that he is behind the times, that he could have done anything he liked with me the first week we met, when I was madly in love with him, that then I was dying for him to ask me to go away with him, and would gladly have made a mess of my life at one word from him—but four weeks later I would rather have died than go away with him.

41

'Only once,' she said, 'I was almost beaten. I fell in love with a stone figure. Women are like sea-gulls, they worship stone figures. ... I went very mad, Dikran. He told me that he didn't deserve being loved by me—he admired me tremendously, you see—because he hadn't it in his poor soul to love anyone. He simply couldn't love, he said ... and he felt such a brute. He said that often, poor boy—he felt such a brute! He passed a hand over his forehead and, with a tragic little English gesture, tried to be articulate, to tell me how intensely he felt that he was missing the best things in life, and yet couldn't rectify it, because ... "Oh, my dear, I'm a hopeless person!" he said despairingly, and I forgot to pity myself in pitying him.

'But he got cold again. He weighed his words carefully: No, he liked me as much as he could like anyone, but he didn't *think* he loved me—mark that glorious, arrogant *think*, Dikran! ... He was very ambitious; with the sort of confident, yet intensive, nerve-racking ambition which makes great men. Very young, very wonderful, brilliantly successful in his career at an age when other men were only beginning theirs—an iron man, with the self-destructive selfishness of ice, which freezes the thing that touches it, but itself melts in the end. ... He froze *me*. Don't think I'm exaggerating, please, but, as he spoke—it was at lunch, and a coon band was playing—I died away all to myself. I just died, and then came to life again, coldly, and bitterly, and despairingly, but still loving him. ... I couldn't *not* love him, you see. His was the sort of beauty that was strong, and vital, and a little contemptuous, and with an English cleanness about it that was scented. ... I am still loyal to my first despairing impression of him. And I knew that I was really in love with him, because I couldn't bear the idea of ever having loved anyone else. I was sixteen again, and worshipped a hero, a man who did things.

'I was a fool, of course—to believe him, I mean. But when women lose their heads they lose the self-confidence and pride of a lifetime, too—and, anyway, it's all rubbish about pride; there isn't any pride in absolute love. There's a name to be made out of a brilliant epigram on love and pride—think it over, Dikran. . . . What an utter fool I was to believe him! As he spoke, over that lunch-table, I watched his grey English eyes, which tried to look straight into mine but couldn't, because he was shy; he was trying to be frightfully honest with me, you see, and being so honest makes decent men shy. He felt such a brute, but he had to warn me that in any love affair with him, he . . . yes, he did love me, in his way, he suddenly admitted. But his way wasn't, couldn't ever be, mine. He simply couldn't give himself wholly to any one, as I was doing. And he so frightfully wanted to—to sink into my love for him. . . . "Shelmerdene, it's all so damnable," he said pathetically, and his sincerity bit into me. But I had made up my mind. I was going to do the last foolish thing in a foolish life—I'm a sentimentalist, you know.

'I believed him. But I clung to my pathetic love affair with both hands, so tight—so tight that my nails were white and blue with their pressure against his immobility. I made up my mind not to let go of him, however desperate, however hopeless . . . it was an attempt at life. He was all I wanted, I could face life beside him. Other men had been good enough to play with, but my stone figure—why, I had been looking for him all my life! But in my dreams the stone figure was to come wonderfully to life when I began to worship it—in actual life my worshipping could make the stone figure do nothing more vital than crumble up bits of bread in a nervous effort to be honest with me! I took him at that—I told you I was mad, didn't I?—I took him at his own value, for as much as I could get out of him.

'I set out to make myself essential to him, mentally, physically, every way. . . . If he couldn't love me as man to women, then he would have to love me as a tree trunk loves the creepers round it; I was going to cling all round him, but without his knowing. But I hadn't much time—just a month or perhaps six weeks. He was under orders for Africa, where he was going to take up a big administrative job, amazing work for so young a man; but then he was amazing. Just a few weeks I had, then, to make him feel that he couldn't bear life, in Africa or anywhere, without me. And, my dear! life didn't hold a more exquisite dream than that which brought a childish flush under my *rouge*, the very dream of dreams, of how, a few days before he went, he would take me in his arms and tell me that he couldn't bear to go alone, and that I must follow him, and together we would face all the scandal that would come of it. . . . I passionately wanted the moment to come when he would offer to risk his career for me; I wanted him to offer me his ambition, and then I would consider whether to give it back to him or not. But he didn't. I lost.

'And I had seemed so like winning during that six weeks between that horrible lunch and his going away! London love affairs are always scrappy, hole-in-the-corner things, but we managed to live together now and again. And then, *mon Dieu!* he suddenly clung to me and said he wasn't seeing enough of me, that London was getting between us, and that we must go away somewhere into the country for at least a week before he left, to breathe and to love. . . . Wouldn't you have thought I was winning? I thought so, and my dreams were no more dreams, but actual, glorious certainties; he would beg me on his knees to follow him to Africa!

'We went away ten days before he sailed, to a delightful little inn a few miles from Llangollen. Seven days we spent there. Wonderful, intimate days round about that little inn by the Welsh stream; we were children playing under a wilderness of blue sky, more blue than Italy's because of the white and grey puffs of clouds which make an English sky more human than any other; and we played with those toy hills which are called mountains in Wales, and we were often silent because there was too much to talk about. . . . And as we sat silently facing each other in the train back to London, I knew I had won. There were three days left.

'In London, he dropped me here at my house, and went on to his flat; he was to come in the evening to fetch me out to dinner. But he was back within an hour. I had to receive him in a kimono. I found him pacing up and down this room, at the far end there, by the windows. He came quickly to me, and told me that his orders had been changed—he had to go to

Paris first, spend two days there, and then to Africa via Marseilles. "To Paris?" I said, not understanding. "Yes, tonight—in two hours," he said, quickly, shyly. He was embarrassed at the idea of a possible scene. But he was cold. He must go at once, he said. And he looked eager to go, to go and be doing. He shook both my hands—I hadn't a word—and almost forgot to kiss me. It was just as though nothing had ever happened between us, as though we hadn't ever been to Wales, or played, and laughed, and loved; as though he had never begged me to run my fingers through his hair, because I had said his hair was a garden where gold and green flowers grew. He was going away; and he was just as when I had first met him, or at that lunch—I hadn't gained anything at all, it was all just a funny, tragic, silly dream ... he had come and now he was going away. He would write to me, he said, and he would be back in sixteen months. ...

'I'm not a bad loser, you know; I can say such and such a thing isn't for me, and then try and undermine my wretchedness with philosophy. But I simply didn't exist for a few months; I just went into my little shell and stayed there, and was miserable all to myself, and not bitter at all, because I sort of understood him, and knew he had been true to himself. It was I who had failed in trying to make him false to his own nature. ... But there's a limit to all things; there comes a time when one can't bear any more gloom, and then there is a reaction. No one with any courage can be wretched for ever—anyway, I can't. So, suddenly, after a few months, I went out into the world again, and played and jumped about, and made my body so tired that my mind hadn't a chance to think.

'His first few letters were cold, honest things, a little pompous in their appreciations of me tacked on to literary descriptions of the Nile, and the desert, and the natives. I wrote to him only once, a wonderful letter, but I hadn't the energy to write again—what was the good?

'At the end of a year I was really in the whirl of the great world again. There were a few kicks left in Shelmerdene yet, I told myself hardly, and Maurice became just a tender memory. I never thought of how he would come back to England soon,

as he had said, and what we would do then, for I had so dinned it into myself that he wasn't for me that I had entirely given up the quest of the Blue Bird. He was just a tender memory . . . and impressionable me fell in love again. But not as with Maurice—I was top-dog this time. He was the sort of man that didn't count except in that I loved him. He was the servant of my reaction against Maurice, and to serve me well he had to help me wipe out all the castles of sentiment I had built around Maurice. And the most gorgeous castle of all I had built round that little Welsh inn! Something must be done about that, I told myself; but for a long time I was afraid of the ghost of Maurice, which might still haunt the place, and bring him back overpoweringly to me. It was a risk; by going there with someone else I might either succeed in demolishing Maurice's last castle, or I might tragically have to rebuild all the others, and worship him again.

'He had continued to write to me, complaining of my silence. And he had somehow become insistent—he missed me, it seemed. He didn't write that he loved me, but he forgot to describe the Nile, and wrote about love as though it were a real and beautiful thing and not a pastime to be wedged in between fishing and hunting. I wrote to him once again, rather lightly, saying that I had patched up my heart and might never give him a chance to break it again. That was just before I went to demolish the last castle of my love for him. For I did go; one day my young man produced a high-powered car which could go fast enough to prevent one sleeping from boredom, and I said "Us for Llangollen," and away we went . . .

'The divinest thing about that little inn was its miniature dining-room, composed almost entirely of a large bow-window and a long Queen Anne refectory table. There were three tables, of which never more than one was occupied. Maurice and I had sat at the table by the window, and now my reaction and I sat there again; we looked out on to a toy garden sloping down to a brown stream which made much more noise than you could think possible for so narrow a thing. My back was to the door, and I sat facing a large mirror, with the garden and the stream on my right; he sat facing the window

46

adoring me, the adventure, the stream, and the food. And I was happy too, for now I realized that I had fallen out of love with Maurice, for his ghost didn't haunt the chair beside me, and I could think of him tenderly, without regret. I was happy —until, in the mirror in front of me, I saw the great figure of Maurice, and his face, at the open door. Our eyes met in the mirror, the eyes of statues, waiting. . . . I don't know what I felt—I wasn't afraid, I know. Perhaps I wasn't even ashamed. I don't know how long he stood there, filling the doorway. Not more than a few seconds, but all the intimacy of six weeks met in our glance in that mirror. At last he took his eyes off mine and looked at the man beside me, who hadn't seen him. I thought his lips twitched, and his eyes became adorably stern, and then the mirror clouded over. . . . When I could see again the door was closed, and Maurice was gone. The magic mirror was empty of all but my unbelieving eyes, and the profile of the man beside me, who hadn't seen him and never knew that I had lived six weeks while he ate a potato. . . .

'I stayed my week out in Wales, because I always try to do what is expected of me. When I got home, right on the top of a pile of letters— I had given orders for nothing, not even wires, to be sent on to me—was a wire, which had arrived one hour after I had left for Wales. It was from Southampton, and it said: "Just arrived. Am going straight up to the little palace in Wales because of memories. Will arrive there dinner-time. Shall we dine together by the window?"

'And so, you see, I had won and lost and won again, but how pathetically. . . . Am I such a bad woman, d'you think?'

As I look back now on the past years, I find that the thing that penetrated most into my inner self, shocked me to the heart, and gave me no room and left no desire for any pretence about the will of fate and destiny, such as sometimes consoles grief, was the death of my friend Louis. Unlike most great friendships, mine with Louis began at school; and those, to whom circumstances have not allowed friendships at school, cannot realize the intensity of certain few friendships which, beginning on a basis of tomfoolery and ragging, as the general relations between schoolboys do begin, yet survive them all, and steadily ripen with the years into a maturity of companionship, which has such a quality and nobility of its own that no other relation, not even that of passionate love, can ever take its place when it is gone.

I have not happened to mention Louis before in these papers for the reason that he had actually come very little into my life in London. In fact, we retained our intimacy against the aggression of our different lives, which was rather paradoxical for the casual people we believed ourselves to be. (Without a sincere belief in his own casualness the modern youth would be the most self-important ass of all generations.) Our ways of life led very contrarily; there was nowhere they could rationally touch; he, a soldier; I, a doctor, lawyer, or pedlar, I did not know which. But I had the grace, or if you like, the foolishness, to envy him the definite markings of his career; I envied him his knowledge of the road he wished to tread, and of the almost certainties which lay inevitably along that road.

Later, in those very best of days, I used to talk about him to Shelmerdene. And as I described, she listened and wondered. For, she said, such a man as I described Louis to be, and myself, could have nothing in common. But I told her that it isn't necessary for two people to have anything 'in common' but friendship—and as I made that meaningless remark I put on a superior air, and she did not laugh at me. She continued to wonder during months, and at last she said, 'Produce this wretched youth.' But I would not produce him, 'because Louis has never in his life met or dreamt of anyone like you, and he will fall in love with you straight away. And as he is more honest than I am, so he will fall in love with you much more seriously, and that will be very bad for him, because you are the sort of woman that you are. It isn't fair to destroy the illusions of a helpless subaltern in the Rifle Brigade. . . . No, I will not produce him, Shelmerdene.' But of course I did, and of course Louis saw, heard, and succumbed delightedly, and all through that lunch and for the half-hour after I had to keep a very stern eye on Shelmerdene and take great care not to let her get within a yard of him, else she would have asked him to go and see her next time he was in town, and then there would have been another wild-eyed ghost wandering about the desert places of Mayfair. As for Louis, he beat even his own record for dullness during that lunch. He admired her tremendously and obviously, and too obviously he couldn't understand a beautiful woman with beauty enough to be as dull as she liked, saying witty and amusing things every few seconds, always giving the most trivial remark, the most stereotyped phrase, such a queer twist as would make it seem delightfully new. For ever after he pestered me to 'produce' her again, and I made myself rather unpopular by putting him off; and I never did let him see her again. On Shelmerdene's part it was just cussedness to worry me to see him again, for with a disgusted laugh at my 'heavy father stunt,' she forgot all about him; after that lunch she had found him 'rather dull and a dear, and much to be loved by all women over thirty-five. I am not yet old enough to love your Louis,' she said. And she retained her surprise at our friendship.

It was, perhaps, rather surprising; surprising not so much that we were friends, but how we ever became friends; for there are many people in this world who could be great friends with each other if they could but once surmount the first barrier, if they could but *wish* to surmount that barrier—and between Louis and me there was much more than a simple

49

barrier to surmount. We became friends in spite of ourselves, then; though Louis, as you may believe, had nothing at all to do with the affair; he just sat tight and let things happen to him, for his was not the nature consciously to defeat an invisible aim, a tyrannical decree. As one of England's governing classes, even at the age of fourteen when I first met him, such a rebellion as that of forcing God's hand about the smallest trifle would somehow have savoured to him of disloyalty to the 'Morning Post,' which, together with the Navy, Louis took as representing the British Empire.

I had been at school already one term when Louis came; and so it was at breakfast on the opening day of the winter term that I first noticed his bewildered face, though as we grew to prefects that same face aired so absolute a nonchalance that, together with my rather sophisticated features, we thoroughly deserved the title of the '*blasted roués.*' However at that time, we were not prefects but 'new bugs,' though Louis was by one term a newer 'bug' than myself and my friends, and therefore had to sit at the bottom of the 'bug' table and take his food as he found it. I, of course, took no notice of him at all; I maintained a, so to speak, official *hauteur* about our meal-time relations—one couldn't do anything else, you know, if one wished to keep unimpaired the dignity of one's seniority. I had, in fact, no use for newer 'bugs' than myself; I was quite happy at my own end of the table with the three men (ages fourteen to fourteen-and-a-half) with whom I shared a study. We made a good and gay study, I remember, for they were three stalwart fellows and I, even at that age not taking my Armenianism very seriously, gave a quite passable imitation of an English public-school man.

How, as I looked round at my three friends and said to myself 'here are companions for life,' how was I to know to the irruption into my life of a bewildered face! I despised that face. It was the face of a newer 'bug' than myself. But the wretched man could play soccer, I noticed; his deft work at 'inside right' to my 'centre forward' warmed my heart; and, by the time the term was half over, he had gained a certain distinction for being consistently at the bottom of the lowest form in the school; one rather liked a man for sticking to his convictions like that.

Nevertheless we became silently inimical. He ceased to look bewildered; with an English cunning he had already found that an air of nonchalance pays best. And his sort of 'Oh, d'you think so?' air began to irritate me; it was no good doing my man of the world on a man who obviously made a point of not believing what I said. I rather felt in speaking to him as an irritated and fussy foreign ambassador must feel before the well-bred imperturbability of Mr Balfour; I wasn't then old enough to know I felt like that, but myself and study had reasonable grounds for deciding that 'that sloppy-haired new bug was a conceited young swine,' and that he was trading rather too much on being at the bottom of the school.

There was a dark-haired, sallow-faced youth, one Marsden, who had come the same term as we three; he had at first shared our study, but had been fired out for being a cub. And, by intimating to the House-Master that if he was put back in our study, new bugs or no, we wouldn't answer for his mother's knowing him, we had fired him out in such a way that he couldn't ever get back. But he didn't try to get back. He just went into the newest bug's study, and there, when Louis came the next term, made firm and fast friends with him. Marsden disliked me much more than he disliked anyone else, as I had been the instigator of his ejection from our study, and so the silent and contemptuous enmity with which Louis eyed me wasn't very strange. Those two made common cause in their indifference to anything we three at the head of the table might say; and soon, things came to such a pass that we had to put lumps of salt into the potato dish before handing it down to them. And even that didn't seem to have much effect, for one tea-time I distinctly heard a murmur resembling 'Armenian Jew' escape from Marsden's lips; that, of course, couldn't be borne, and I couldn't then explain to him that there was no such person as an Armenian Jew, for I wasn't quite certain about it—all I knew was that I wasn't a Jew, and it wasn't Marsden who was going to call me one in vain. So there and then I upped and threw my pot of jam at his head, striking him neatly just above the right eye. I didn't do it in anger; I didn't know why I did it, though now I know it was done through a base passion for notoriety, which I still have, though in a less primitive manner. I certainly got notoriety then, and also six cuts from a very supple cane and a Georgic on which to work off my ardour.

But I gained Louis for a friend. He had, it seemed, admired the deft and unassuming way in which I had thrown that pot of jam—he knew even less than I did about that passion for notoriety—and when he met me in the passage as I came back from my six cuts in the prefects' room, he said, 'I say, bad luck,' and I suggested that if his friend Marsden's ugly face hadn't got in the way of a perfectly harmless pot of jam I wouldn't have got a licking. Thus, in a three-minute talk, we became friends; but when we each went to our own studies we didn't know we were friends—in fact, I was quite prepared to go on treating him as an enemy until, when we met again, we both seemed to find that we had something to say to each other. And throughout those years of school we had always something to say to each other which we couldn't say quite in the same way to anyone else, and that seems to me to be the basis of all friendship. . . . I don't quite know what happened to Marsden, or how Louis told him that he had decided to discontinue his friendship. I have an idea that Marsden went on disliking me through four years of school, and that if I met him on Piccadilly tomorrow would recognize me only to scowl at me, the man who not only hit him over the eye with a pot of jam, but also deprived him of his best friend.

Louis and I left school together; he on his inevitable road to Sandhurst, and I, with a puckered side glance at Oxford, to Edinburgh University. Even now I don't know why I went to Edinburgh and not to Oxford; I had always intended going to Oxford, my family had always intended that I should go to Oxford, up to the last moment I was actually going to Oxford —when, suddenly, with a bowler hat crammed over my left ear and a look of vicious obstinacy, I decided that I would go to Edinburgh instead.

Of course it was a silly mistake. The only thing I have

gained by not going to Oxford is an utter inability to write poetry and a sort of superior contempt for all pale, interesting-looking young men with dark eyes and spiritual hair who are tremendously concerned about the utter worthlessness of Mr William Watson's poetry. Of course my own superior attitude may be just as unbearable as their anæmic enthusiasm over, say, a newly discovered *rondel* by the youngest son of the local fishmonger; but I at least do sincerely try to face and appreciate literature boldly and frankly, and normally, and not self-consciously as they do, attacking literature from anywhere but a sane standpoint, trying to force a breach in any queer spot so that it is unusual and has not been thought of before; and through this original breach will suddenly appear an Oxford face with a queer unhallowed grin of self-conscious cleverness; and all this for a thin book of poems in a yellow cover, called, as like as not, 'Golden Oxygen!'

Louis, down at Sandhurst, was being made into a soldier, and I, up at Edinburgh, was on the high road to general fecklessness. I only stayed there a few months; jumbled months of elementary medicine, political economy, meta-physics, theosophy—I once handed round programmes at an Annie Besant lecture at the Usher Hall—and beer, lots of beer. And then, one night, I emptied my last mug, and with another side-glance at Oxford, came down to London—'to take up a literary career' my biographer will no doubt write of me. I may of course have had a 'literary career' at the back of my mind, but as it was I slacked outrageously, much to Louis' disgust and envy. I have already written of those months, how I walked in the Green Park, and sat in picture galleries, and was lonely.

That first loneliness was lightened only by the occasional visits to London of Louis. He was by now a subaltern in the Rifle Brigade, with an indefinite but cultured growth some-where between his nose and upper lip, and a negligent way of wearing mufti, as though to say, 'God, it's good to be back in civilized things again!' They were jolly, sudden evenings, those! London was still careless then. Of an evening a couple of young men in dress suits, with top hats balanced over their

eyebrows and eyes full of a *blasé* vacancy, were not as remarkable as they now are. Life has lost its whilom courtesy to a top hat. Red flags and top hats cannot exist side by side; the world is not big enough for both. Ah, thou Bolshevik, thou class-beridden shop-steward! When ye die, how can ye say that ye have ever lived if, in your aggressive experiences, you have not known upon your foreheads the elegant weight of a top hat, made especially to suit your Marxian craniums by one Locke, who has an ancient shop at the lower end of St. James's Street and did at one time dictate the headwear of the beaux of White's and Crockford's. I warrant the life of my top hat, made by that same artist to withstand the impact of the fattest woman on earth, against all the battering eloquence of all the orators in all the Albert Halls of the all Red Flag countries. With it on my head I will finesse any argument whatsoever with you any night of the week. And at the end of the argument, if you are still obstinate, I will cram my blessed top hat on your head and, lo and behold! you are at once a Labour Minister in the Cabinet, and a most respectable man with a most rectangular house in Portland Square! . . . But I must go back to Louis, who never got further in his study of Labour than an idea that all station-masters were labour leaders because they took tips so impressively.

Those occasional evenings were very good. I put away from myself writing and books—Louis hadn't really ever read anything but Kipling, 'Ole-Luk-Oie' and 'The Riddle of the Sands'—and I temporarily forgot Shelmerdene, and we dined right royally. I don't know what we talked about, perhaps we talked of nothing at all; but we talked all the time, and we laughed a great deal, and we still had the good old '*blasted roué*' touch about us. We were very, very old indeed, so old that we decided that the first act of no play or revue in the world could compensate one for a hurried dinner; and we were old enough to know that a confidential manner to *maîtres d'hôtels* is a thing to be cultivated, else a chicken is apt to be wizened and the sweet an unconscionable long time in coming. After dinner, a show, and then perhaps a night club, 'to teach those gals how to dance.'

We founded a Club for Good Mannered People. I, as the founder, was the president of the club, and Louis the vice-president; there were no members because we unanimously black-balled everyone whom, in a moment of weakness, one or other of us might propose. We decided, in the end, that the Club could never have any members except the president and vice-president, simply because the men of our own generation were the worst mannered crew God ever put within lounging distance of a drawing-room. ... There must be something wrong, we said, in a world where public-school men could be recognized by the muddy footprints they left on other people's carpets. So it was obviously left to us to supply the deficiency of our generation, both as regards manners and everything else. We made a cult of good manners; Louis took to them as a cult where he had never taken to them as a necessity, and the happiest moments of his life were when he could work it off on to some helpless woman who had dropped an umbrella or a handkerchief. The Club, we decided, must never come to an end; it must go on being a Club until one or other of us should die. ... and now the Club is no more, for suddenly a spring gave way, the world gave a lurch towards hell, and Louis stopped playing at soldiers to go away and be a real soldier, to die in his first attack with a bullet in his chest. ...

CHAPTER 9

SOMEWHERE in these papers I have said that Shelmerdene left England, but I touched on it very lightly, for I am only half-heartedly a realist, and may yet live to be accused of shuffling humanity behind a phrase. . . . Youth must endure its periods of loneliness with what grace it can; and youth could endure them as resignedly as its preceptors, if it were not for its grotesque self-importance, which inflates loneliness to such a size that it envelops a young man's whole being, leaving him at the end a sorry wreck of what was once a happy mortal. Anyway, that is what happened to me; I took the whole affair in the worst possible spirit, and, during that probation time to wisdom, thought and wrote and did so many silly things, smashed ideals and cursed idols with such morbid thoroughness and conviction (after the fashion of all the bitterest young men), that I must have been as detestable a person as ever trickled wheezily from the, well, pessimistic pen of a Mr Wyndham Lewis. . . . But it takes very little effort to forget that time entirely, to let it bury itself with what mourning it can muster from the Shades which sent it to plague me. Enough that it passed, but not before it had, as they say, 'put me wise' about the world and its ways.

For Shelmerdene had left behind her much more than just loneliness; much that was more precious and, thankfully, more lasting; for she had found a young man, shaped entirely of acute angles and sharp corners, and had rubbed and polished them over with such delicate tact that it was only months after she had gone that I suddenly realized how much more fit I was to cope with a complicated world since I had known her. But, more importantly, Shelmerdene to me was England. Before I met her I did not know England; I knew English, but England only as a man knows the landmarks about him in a strange country. But when she had come and gone England was a discovered country, a vast and ever-increasing panorama in which discoveries were continually made, leaving yet more hidden valleys of discoveries still to be made—and to be enjoyed! So much and much more, O unbeliever, I learnt from Shelmerdene, and in the learning of it lay the best and gladdest lesson of all.

Time, they say, can efface all things, but in truth it can efface nothing but its own inability to smooth out the real problems of life; so at least I have found in the one instance in which I have challenged time to do its best for me, a slave bound down by an unholy wizardry; or else, perhaps, it was that Shelmerdene was not made of the stuff which fades into the years and becomes musty and haggard in their increasing company. I do not know. But, take it as I will, all the service time has been able to do for me has been negative, for without disarranging one hair of her head it has only emphasized in me the profound and subtle influence of that gracefully licentious woman whom I once called Shelmerdene, because, I told her, 'it is the name of an American girl which I found in a very bad American novel about the fanatical Puritans of New England, and the name seems to suit you because in New England they would have treated you exactly as they treated Shelmerdene Gray, the heroine of this book, whom they branded and burnt as a shameless woman, but loved in their withered hearts for her gaiety, and elegance, and wit, which they couldn't understand, but vaguely felt was as much an expression of Christ as their own wizened virtue.'

Out of the silence of two years at last came a letter from her. I found it when I came in very late one night, and for a long time I stood in my little hall and examined the Eastern stamp and postmark; and the writing on the envelope was so exactly the same as on the last note she had sent me before leaving England that I had to smile at the idea of Shelmerdene, in the rush of her last pursuit of her perfect fate, laying in a sufficient store of her own special nibs to last her for the lifetime she intended to spend abroad; for when I opened the letter I found that, as I had guessed, she would never come back to England, saying, 'I am a fugitive branch which has at last found its parent tree. . . . I have run my perfect fate to earth, Dikran! more perfect than any dream, more lasting than the

57

most perfect dream. And life is so beautiful that I can scarcely bear your not being here to share it, for, you see, I am quite sure that you are still the dear you were two years ago. But it is so tiresome of you to be so young, and to have to experience so many things before you can qualify for my sort of happiness; and on top of being young you are so restless and fussy, too, with your ideas of what you are going to do, and your ambitions—how it must tire the mind to be ambitious! It would certainly tire mine in this climate, so will you please make a note of the fact that I simply forbid you to come out here to join me! You are too young to be happy, and you aren't wise enough to be contented; and you can't hope to be wise enough until you begin to lose a bit of that mane of hair of yours, which I hope you never will, for I remember how I loved one particular wave in it in the far-off age when I thought I was in love with you. . . . It is terrible, but I am forgetting England. Terrible, because it must be wrong to forget one's country, seeing how you oppressed nationalities go on remembering your wretched countries for centuries of years, and throwing bombs and murdering policemen for all the world as though you weren't just as happy as everyone else, while I, with a country, which is after all worth remembering, go and forget it after a paltry two years! Of course it will always be my country, and I shall always love it for the good things it has given me, but as a *fact* in my life it has faded into something more dim than a memory. A spell has been put upon me, Dikran, to prevent a possible ache in my heart for the things I was born among, a spell which has made me forget Europe and all my friends in it except just you, and you because, in spite of all your English airs, you will always be a pathetic little stranger in a very strange land, fumbling for the key. . . . Ah, this wise old East of mine! so old and so wise, my dear, that it knows for certain that nothing is worth doing; and as you happen, perhaps, on the ruins of a long-dead city by the desert, you can almost hear it chuckling to itself in its hard-earned wisdom, as though to say that since God Himself is that very same Law which creates men, and cities, and religions only to level them into the dust of the roads and the sands of the desert, why fight against God? It is a corrupt and deadening creed, this of the East, but it has a weight of ancestral will behind it which forces you to believe in it; and belief in it leaves you without your Western defences, and open to be charmed into non-resistance, as I and my Blue Bird have been charmed, else perhaps I would not now be so happy, and might even be dining with you on the terrace of the Hyde Park Hotel. . . . Rather bitterly you have often called me the slave of Ishtar, though at the time I did not know who the lady was, for I was always rather weak about goddesses and such-like; but I guessed she had something to do with love because of the context, for you were developing your pleasant theory about how I would come to a bad end, someday. . . . Well, Dikran, that "someday" of your prophecy has come. I've never belonged so wholly to Ishtar as I do now that I am perhaps in the very same country in which she once haunted the imagination of the myriad East. I've made a mess of life, I've come to my bad end, and, as I tell you, I have never known such perfect happiness. The world couldn't wish me a worse fate, and I couldn't wish myself a better. . . . Don't write to me, please. I can always imagine you much more clearly than your letters can express you, and if I think of you as doing big things, as I pray you may, it will be better for me than knowing that you are doing nothing at all, which might easily happen, seeing how lazy you are. . . . In the dim ages I was all wrong about life. For I know now that restraint in itself is the most perfect emotion. . . .'

I laid the letter down, and as the windows were already greying with the March dawn it did not seem worth while going to a sleepless bed; and so I sat on in my chair, drawing my overcoat round me for warmth, and smoked many cigarettes. I felt very old indeed, for was not that letter the echo of a long-dead experience, and are not long-headed experiences the peculiar property of old men? No visions of the Shelmerdene of that letter came up to disturb my peace, for she did not fit in with my ideas of the East, she had never appealed to that Eastern side which must be somewhere in me, but had always been to me a perfect symbol of the grace and kindliness and devilry of the arrogant West. I could not see her as she described herself, happy, meditative, wise in contentment. . . . Her contentment is too much like an emotion, and therefore spurious, I thought, and so she will still dine with me on the terrace of the Hyde Park Hotel, and will wonder why I look so differently at her, for I will still be young while she will be middle-aged. . . . No, that letter conjured up no perfect vision of her in the East, except that I saw her, melodramatically perhaps, pleading on her knees for release from the bonds of Ishtar, for I knew that not even a Shelmerdene among women can evade the penalty of so many unsuccessful love-affairs just by the success of one.

The grey of the March dawn became paler, and the furniture and books in my room seemed so wan and unreal that I thought drowsily that they were a dream of last night and were fading before the coming daylight; and later, when my thoughts had mellowed into a security of retrospect, I may have slept, for I realized with a start that the maid had come in to tidy up the room for breakfast, but had got no further than the door, perhaps wondering whether I had been very drunk the night before, or only just 'gay.'

Retrospect came naturally after that letter, for she had written at the end how she had found the true worth of 'restraint;' it would have been just a phrase in a letter if I had not remembered, as she must have when she wrote it, that the word had a context, and that the context lay in a long summer afternoon on a silent reach of the river many miles from Maidenhead. . . . One day that summer I had suggested to her that, as the world was becoming a nuisance with its heat and dust, we might go and stay on the river for a few days, but she had said, quite firmly, 'No, I can't do that. I am not yet old enough to put my name down for the divorce stakes, so if you don't mind, Dikran, we will call that bet off and think of something else. For if that same husband heard of my staying on the river with a young man of uncelibate eye and uncertain occupation, he would at once take steps about it, and although I like you well enough as a man, I couldn't bear you as a co-respondent. . . . But if you really do want to stay on the river, I will get the Hartshorns to ask us both down, for they have a delightful house on a little hill, from which you can see the twilight creeping over the Berkshire downs across the river.'

'Oh, we can't do that,' I said; 'Guy Hartshorn is such a stiffnecked ass and his wife is dull enough to spoil any river—'

'Tolerance, my dear, is what you lack,' she said, 'tolerance and a proper understanding of the relation between a stiffnecked ass and a possible host. And Guy, poor dear, always does his duty by his guests. . . . Please don't be silly about it, Dikran. The Hartshorns distinctly need encouragement as hosts, so you and I will go down and encourage them. And if you can manage to cloak your evil thoughts behind a hearty manner and watch Guy as he swings a racing punt down the river, you will learn more about punting and the reason why Englishmen are generally considered to be superior to foreigners than I could teach you in a lifetime.'

We had been two days at the house on the little hill by the river (for, of course, we went there) before, on the third afternoon, after lunch, our chance came, and Shelmerdene and I were at last alone on the river; I had not the energy to do more than paddle very leisurely and look from here to there, but always in the end to come back to the woman who lay facing me against the pale green cushions of the Hartshorn punt, steeped in the happy sunshine of one of those few really warm days which England now and again manages to steal from the molten South, and exhibits in a new green and golden loveliness. From round a bend of the river we could quite clearly see the ivy-covered Georgian house of our host, perched imperiously up on the top of its little hill, but not imperiously enough to prevent the outlet of two days' impatience in the curse I vented on it.

'Little man with little toy wants big toy of the same pattern and cries when he can't have it,' she mocked me, and smiled away my bad temper, which had only a shallow root in impatience. But I would not let it go all at once, for man is allowed licence on summer afternoons on the river, and I challenged her to say if she did not know of better ways of spending the whole glorious time between dinner and midnight than by playing bridge, 'as we tiresomely do at the house on the hill, much to the delight of that sombre weeping elm which looks in at the window and can then share the burden of its complaining leaves with my pessimistic soul.'

'We will leave your soul severely alone for the moment, but as for playing bridge, I think it is very good for you,' she said. 'It is very good for you to call three No Trumps, and be doubled by someone who won't stand any nonsense, and go down four hundred or so. It teaches you restraint.'

'Restraint,' I said, 'is the Englishman's art of concealing his emotions in such a way that everyone can guess exactly what they are. And I have acquired it so perfectly that you know very well that only the other day you told me how you admired my restraint, and how I would never say to a man's face what I couldn't say just as well behind his back.' But she did not answer, and in silence I pulled into a little aimless backwater, and moored by a willow which let through just enough sun to speck Shelmerdene's dress with bright arabesques.

I changed my seat for the cushions and lay full length in front of Shelmerdene, but it was as though she had become part of the river, she was so silent. I said something, I can't remember what it was, but it must have suited the day and my mood. I could not see her face because she had turned it towards the bank and it was hidden under the brim of her pale blue hat; but when my words had broken the quietness and she turned it towards me, I was surprised at the firm set of her lips and the sadness of her smile.

'You are making love to me, and that is quite as it should be,' she said. 'But on the most beautiful of all days I have the saddest thoughts, for though you laughed at me when I talked about restraint, I was really very serious indeed. I know a lot about restraint, my dear, and how the lack of it can make life suddenly very horrible . . . for once upon a time I killed an old man because I didn't know the line between my desires and his endurance.' She shook her head at me gently. 'No, that won't do, Dikran. You were going to say something pretty about my good manners, but that is all so much play-acting, and, besides, good manners are my trade and profession, and without them I should long ago have been down and under, as I deserve to be much more than Emma Hamilton ever did. .... The tragedy about people like me is that we step into life at the deep end and find only the shallow people there, and when we meet someone really deep and very sincere, like that old man, we rather resent it, for we can't gauge him by the standards we use for each other. Men like that bring a sudden reality into life, but the reality is unacceptable and always ugly because it is forced upon one, while the only realities that are beautiful are those that were born in your heart when you were born; just like your country for you, which you have never seen and may never see, and yet has been your main reality in life since you were born; a reality as sad and beautiful as the ancestral memories which must lurk somewhere in you, but which you can't express because you have not learnt yet how to be really natural with yourself. And when you have learnt that you will have learnt the secret of great writing, for literature is the natural raw material which every man secretes within himself, but only a few can express it to the world. But I may be wrong about all that, and anyway you must know a great deal more about great thinking and great writing than I do, for you have read about it in dull books while I have only sensed it in my trivial way. ....'

'Shelmerdene, I want to hear about your old man,' I said, 'whom you say you killed. But that is only your way of saying that he was in love with you, and that you hurt him so much that he died of it.'

'Ah, if it had been only that I would not be so sad this afternoon! In fact, I would not be sad at all, for he was old and had to die, and all that about love and being hurt is fair and open warfare. But it was something much beastlier than that, something animal in me, which will make me ashamed whenever I think of that day when we three gave our horses rein down to the Breton coast, and I turned on the old man, a very spitfire of a girl broken loose from the restraint of English generations, forgetting for one fierce moment that her saddle was not covered with the purple of a Roman Augusta, and that she couldn't do as she liked in a world of old men. ... Have you ever seen a quarrel, a real quarrel, Dikran? When someone is so bitterly and intensely angry that he loses all hold on everything but his wretched desire to hurt, and unchains a beast which in a second maims him as deeply as his enemy—no, it maims him more.

'The old Frenchman was my guardian,' she said, 'and the last of a name which you can find here and there in Court Memoirs, in the thick of that riot of gallantry and intrigue which passed for life at old Versailles. But the world has grown out of that and does things much better now, for gallantry has been scattered to the four winds of democracy and is the navvy's part as much as the gentleman's, while intrigue has become the monopoly of the few darling old men who lead governments, more as a way of amusing their daughters than for any special purpose of their own. But if the world has grown old since then so had my old man, for he was none of your rigid-minded *ci-devant aristos* whom you can see any day at the Ritz keeping up appearances on an occasional cocktail and the use of the hotel notepaper; but the air of the *grand seigneur* hadn't weathered proscriptions and revolutions for nothing, and so still clung rather finely to him in spite of himself, and made him seem as old and faded as his ancestors in the world in which he had to live, poor old dear! It was cruel of that other nice old gentleman above him to put him through the ordeal, for he did so bitterly and genuinely resent a world in which honour was second to most things and above nothing. He couldn't forgive, you see. He couldn't forgive himself, nor France, nor God, but especially he couldn't forgive France. Sedan, revolution, republic—and no Turenne or Bonaparte to thrash a Moltke with the flat of his sword, for he wasn't worth more! And all a France could muster were the trinkets of her *monde* and *demi-monde*, and a threatening murmur of "*revanche*" and "*Alsace-Lorraine*"—as though threats and hatred could wipe out the memory of that day of surrender at Sedan, when he stood not ten yards away among only too polite

Prussian aides-de-camp while Napoleon put the seal on his last mistake, and signed away an empire. ... And allowing for exaggeration, and the white-hot excitement to which folk who fuss about honour, etc., are liable, there may have been something in his point of view about it all, for I once heard a man with a lot of letters behind his name say that when a country gives up a limb it also gives up its body; but he may have been wrong, for, after all, France is still France!

'But you would have adored my old man, Dikran, just as I did. He treated life, and men and women with all that etiquette which you so admire; he was simply bristling with etiquette—a deal too much of it for my taste, for I was only seventeen then and liked my freedom like any other Englander. ... But I'm finding it very difficult to describe the man he was, my dear, for in our slovenly sort of English we've got used to describing a person by saying he is like another person, and I can't do that in this case because he belongs as much to a past age as Hannibal, and there isn't anyone like him now. And even when he was alive there were very few—two or three old men as fierce and unyielding and vital as himself, who used to come and dine, and say pretty things to little me who sat at the end of the table with very large eyes and fast-beating heart, wondering why they weren't all leading Cabinets and squashing revolutions, for they seemed to know the secrets of every secret cabal and camarilla in Europe.

'Yes, my old guardian was a remnant of an empire—but what a remnant! Such a fierce-looking little man he was, with pale, steel-blue eyes which pierced into you from under a precipice of a forehead, a bristling Second Empire moustache, and thin bloodless lips which parted before the most exquisite French I've ever heard; I can scarcely bear it when you say I talk French divinely, for I know how pitiful mine is compared to the real thing as done by that old man and Sarah Bernhardt, for they were very old friends and she used often to come and lunch with us.

'He talked well, too, and all the better for having something to say, as well he might have since he had been everything and known everyone worth knowing of his time—ministers, and rebels, and artists, and all the best-known prostitutes of the day; but they did those things better then, Dikran. In fact, more as an excuse for getting away from a parvenu Paris than from any Bonapartist feelings, for he was always an Orleanist. I think he had represented Louis Napoleon at every city which could run to an Embassy from London to Pekin; from where he brought back that ivory Buddha which is on my writing-table, and which has an inscription in ancient Chinese saying that every man is his own god, but that Buddha is every man's God, which goes a long way to prove that the wisdom of the East wasn't as wise as all that, after all.

'But you are getting restless,' she said suddenly. 'You probably want to open the tea-basket to see what's inside, or you've just seen a water rat—'

'No, it's a little more subtle than that, Shelmerdene, although as a fact I do see a water-rat not a yard from you on the bank. . . . I merely wanted to know how it was that, since you had a perfectly good father alive in England, you were allowed to go gadding about in France with a guardian, soi-disant—'

'We will ignore your soi-disant, young man. But I'll allow your interruption for it may seem a bit complicated. . . . It was like this: as the fortunes of our family had run rather to seed through generations of fast women and slow horses, my father, who was utterly a pet, succumbed to politics for an honest living, or, if you pull a face like that about it, for a dishonest living. For up to that time, in spite of having exactly the figure for it, he had always refused to enter Parliament, because his idea was that the House was just a club, and one already belonged to so many better clubs. But once there nothing could stop him, and when he entered for the Cabinet stakes he simply romped home with a soft job and a fat income. . . . But all that is really beside the point, for between politics and guineas father and I had had a slight disagreement about a certain young man whom I was inclined to marry offhand, being only sixteen, you know, and liking the young man— and, of course, my father did the correct thing, as he always did, gave the young man a glass of port and told him not to be

66

an ass, and shipped me off to Paris to his very old friend. You see, he knew about that old Marquis, and how I'd be quite safe in his care, for any young man who as much as looked at me would have a pair of gimlet eyes asking him who the devil he might be and why he chose to desecrate a young lady's virginal beauty by his so fatuous gaze.

'I've been saying a lot of nice things about that old man to you, but I didn't feel quite like that about him at the time. I liked him, of course, because he was a man; but all that French business about the sanctity of a young maid's innocence got badly on my nerves, for innocence was never my long suit even from childhood, having ears to hear and eyes to see; and I soon began to get very bored with life as my old Frenchman saw it. So it wasn't surprising that I broke out now and again just to shock him, he was so rigid; but I was always sorry for it afterwards because he just looked at me and said not a word for a minute or so, and then went on talking as though I hadn't hurt him—but I had, Dikran! I had hurt him so much that for the rest of the day he often couldn't bear to see me. ... But though I was ashamed of myself for hurting him, I couldn't stop; life with him was interesting enough in a way, of course, but it left out so much, you see; it entirely left out the stupendous fact that I was almost a woman, and a very feminine one at that, who liked an odd young man about now and again just to play about with. But I wasn't allowed any young men, except a twenty-five-year-old over-manicured Vicomte who was so unbearably worldly and useless that I wanted to hit him on the head with my guardian's sword-stick, which he always carried about with him as a sort of mental solace, I think. No, there weren't any young men, nor any restaurants, for the old man simply ignored them; my dear, there wasn't anything at all in my young life except a few old dukes, and dowagers, and the aforesaid young Vicomte, who had manicured himself out of existence and was considered harmless. And so Paris was a dead city to me who lived in the heart of it, and all the more dead for the faded old people who moved about in my life, and tried to change my heart into a Louis-Quinze drawing-room hung with just enough beautiful and musty tapestries to keep out the bourgeois sunshine and carelessness, which I so longed for.

'So I had to amuse myself somehow. . . . I was a bad young woman then, as I am a bad woman now, Dikran; for I've always had a particular sort of vanity which, though it doesn't show on the surface like most silly women's, is deep down in me and has never left me alone; a sort of vanity which makes itself felt in me only in the off seasons when no one happens to be in love with me and I in love with no one, and tells me that I must be dull and unattractive, utterly insignificant and non-existent; it is a weakness in me, but much stronger than I am, for I've never resisted it, but been only too glad to fall in love again as soon as I could; and that is why I've never made a stand against my impressionableness, why I've never run away from or scotched a love-affair which I knew wouldn't last two weeks, however much I loved the wretched man at the time; it was so much the line of least resistance, it drowned that infernal whisper in me that I was of no account at all in the world. But the tragedy of it was, and is, my dear, that indulgence made the monster grow; it was like a drug, for as soon as the off season came again it was at its old tricks with twice its old virulence and malice, and, of course, I gave way again. And so on and so on—did you murmur *dies irae*, Dikran? Well, perhaps, but who knows? There's a Perfect Fate for everyone in this world, and if anyone deserves to find it, it's myself who has failed to find it so often. . . .

'At that time that wretched vanity of mine was only a faint whisper, but there it was, and it had to be satisfied, or else I should have become a good woman, which never did attract me very much. I simply had to amuse myself somehow—and so I formed *la grande idée* of my young life, just as Napoleon III had long ago formed his equally *grande idée* about Mexico and Maximilian, and with the same disastrous results. True, there was no young man about, but there was a man anyway, and a Marquis to boot, even though he was a bit old and rigid. But it was exactly that rigidity of his which I wanted to see about; I wanted to find out things, and in my own way, don't you see? And so, deliberately and with all the malice in me, I

68

set out to subdue the old man. Not childishly and gushingly, although I was so young, but with all the finesse of the eternal game, for clever women are born with *rouge* on their cheeks.

'But it was a disappointing business; I didn't seem to make the impression I wanted to make; all my finesse went for nothing, except as signs or the affection of a ward. Obviously, I thought hopelessly, I don't know all there is to be known about subduing old French marquises, and I had almost decided to try some other amusement when one May morning, a few months after my father had died and appointed him as my guardian and executor, he came into my little boudoir, looking more stern and adorable than ever. And as he came in I knew somehow that big things were coming into my little life; I don't know how, but I knew it as surely as I knew that for all his grand air of calmness he was as shy as any school-boy.

' "My child," he said very gently, "I am intruding on you only because I have something to say to you of the utmost importance and delicacy. I am too old and too much of the world to do things by impulse, and so if I seem to offend against your unworldliness now it is not because I have not thought very carefully about what I am going to say. . . . And I beg you not to count it as any more than the suggestion of an old man who thinks only of your good, and to tell me quite frankly at the end what you think of it.

' "My old friend, your father," he said, "honoured me by placing you entirely in my charge as guardian and executor; but on looking into matters I find that he has left very little for me to do in the latter capacity—very little, in fact, besides that small estate in Shropshire which is entailed on you and your children, as with all its associations of that beautiful girl—scarcely older than you are now, your mother—your father could not bear the thought of it ever passing to strangers. And so, my child, without any reflection on my friend, when you leave my care you enter the world with an old enough name to ensure your position, but without the income to maintain it, and, if you will forgive me, a quite insignificant *dot*; though in your case, as in your beautiful mother's," he added, with his

69

little gallant smile, the first and last of that morning, "a *dot* would be the requirement of a blind man."

' "All this preamble must seem very aimless and tiresome to you, but I wish to put all the facts before you, my dear, before asking you to take the responsibility, as indeed it is, of weighing the suggestion I am going to make. ... You must have seen that I am out of sympathy with this modern world of yours, that I belong to some other period, better or worse, what does it matter? And this world, my child, has little use for those hard-headed persons who cannot change the bent of their minds according to its passing whims, and so it has little use for me who cannot and will not change. ... Do you understand? I mean that I am an old man who is every day losing touch with life, and that I know here, quite certainly, that I have only a very few more years to live. Do not look sad, child," he said, almost impatiently, "it is not that I am complaining, but that I wish you to understand my thoughts. ... Into an old life you have come like a ray of sunshine which is even now making light of your little puzzled frown; and I have a debt of gratitude to pay to you, my child, which I wish to pay at the expense even of your young peace of mind this morning. Although this new world has passed out of my grasp, and will soon pass out of my understanding, I know that it is the proper setting for you, the only subtle and beautiful thing that I have found in it; and my greatest wish is to leave you in a position worthy of your beauty and intelligence. It is not that I am afraid for you, for you are no trivial chit of a girl, but merely that I wish to leave you both happy and independent. . . . And, as it is, I can do nothing, nothing at all! For it has been a fixed rule of our family that we may not leave our fortune and property to anyone who does not bear our name, and thus, though my nephew and I have had no occasion to meet for some fifteen years, I must leave him such money as I have and all this not unappreciated furniture. . . . And that is why, my child, because of my wish to leave you all I have, I have been forced to suggest the only alternative—for I would not have even considered it otherwise—that you should consent to bear my name with me for the few years I have to live, and then, as a young and beautiful widow of means, and bearing an old French name which may still be worth a little consideration, you can take your fit position in the world in which you, and not I, were born to be happy. . . ."

'There it is, Dikran, or as much of it as I can remember. And do you need a setting for it? Oh yes, you do, for you are a little lost. Imagine then, sitting by a window of a large house in the *Rue Colbert*, a young girl with a tattered copy of Madame Bovary skilfully hidden beside her, and a little erect old man, very stiff but *soigné*, and cruelly aged by the sunlight which poured blessedly into the room, standing by the arm of her chair, asking her to marry him. Oh! but you can't imagine it, you will think of him as pleading, and of me as surprised. He didn't plead, he couldn't, and I, my dear, by the time he had finished, wasn't surprised. . . . I knew, you see. Why, I knew everything! Lexicons and encyclopædias had toppled off their dusty shelves, and the Sibylline books had come running to my feet, and the whole world had come trotting out with its wisdom, wisdom as clear and cold as any Dân-nan-Rón that your friend Gloom ever played on his *feadan*, and all in the few minutes that an old man was speaking to me! Of course, it should all have happened differently; I should have been just a "trivial chit of a girl," and then I would have accepted all the old darling said, and gaped, and cried, and said "thank you." But as it was I did none of those things; I'm not quite sure what I did, unless it was nothing at all. . . . It all seems rather mixed now, but on that May morning it was as clear as the sunlight in my cruel young mind—how young and how cruel, Dikran!

'You see, as he spoke, he opened out the world which he so despised to me; page by page he showed me life, how beastly and how beautiful; he showed me both sides, because he himself was both beastly and beautiful . . . And I gloried in it all! At my knowledge and the power it gave me over life. After a while the old man didn't seem to matter—there he was, talking away! I knew about him, and just how beastly and beautiful he was. For he *was* beautiful in his sincerity; I knew that he wished for my good, that to leave me well provided was the only condition he made with death; but I knew too that there was a beastly little imp somewhere in him, as in other men, which turned his finest thoughts into so much bluff, which told him through the locked and bolted doors of his honour that he wanted me for my own sake, and just for that, because I was young and because he loved me, and, stripped of all his honour and guardianship, because he loved me just as Solomon loved his wives, and Lucifer loved Lilith, and as you love me now....

'There it was, then, the whole damnable world, and I, only eighteen, in the middle of it! And there he was, my dear old man, more rigid and more adorable than ever; for, cruel as I was in seeing through him, I loved him all the more for his sweet *naïveté* and for his old, so old illusions about his motives. While as for being shocked at the way he loved me, I've never been shocked by anything but the vulgarity and the indecencies of respectable people, who seem to think that sex is purely a sort of indoor sport to be indulged in darkness and behind barricaded doors, while it is really a setting for the most beautiful Bacchanal that was ever devised by the fairest and purest of God's children. In spite of bibles and the Bishop of London, Mary knew what she was about, Dikran. Love doesn't grow anywhere, to be picked up by the wayside. Pure beauty grows only where beauty already is. . . .

'But, wise as I was, I didn't know what to say; what could I say? He was waiting; I had to say, do something. I did—flung my arms round his neck and told him he was a pet to be so nice to me, and that I must think about it. For the first time that he had wanted me to behave like a woman I behaved consciously like a child—it seemed the easiest way out. And I think he saw that I was acting; he had expected something else, for he smiled very sadly down at me, and patted my hair, saying I was a sweet child not to be angry with him for making life so suddenly serious, and then, very gently, he went away, leaving me in the sunshine, a playmate of the gods . . . And yet I was so sorry for him that I almost cried when I thought of him sitting alone and lonely in his library.

We never spoke of it again. At first it was as though he was waiting for me to say yes, or no, or something, but I didn't say anything, and, later, he seemed to forget. I didn't do it out of cruelty, my dear; I simply couldn't say anything, that's all. After sunshine, rain, you know; I was dismal, frightened of him a little. The romance of that May morning when he had come to me in my room had become a ridiculous fantasy, so that it seemed to me that any reference to it would rather tarnish the very splendid dignity which he had kept, and sort of increased, through it all. Besides, anyway, what was there to say? I had made up my mind as he spoke that morning, through all the clearness of my new-found knowledge. I had never a doubt as to what I was going to do. It wasn't in me to do as he asked, or rather, as he advised, the old dear! I wish it had been in me, for to be a rich French marquise without a marquis is no bad fate for any girl, and it might have helped me to steer clear of many complications. But I couldn't, because all my life, Dikran, I've been cursed by an utter inability to make any money out of love. And that is why I would never be a success in my mother's country of America, where men throw pearls and beauty roses about as a matter of course and are very offended if one suggests an economical flirtation on a gross of diamonds and a hundredweight of Russian sables. . . . It isn't that I am mean-minded, but I cannot take presents from men who love me, for, after all, the old Marquis' offer was a present. When I see other women with relays of fur coats, and pearl necklaces, and no visible means of support, I am thoroughly sorry for myself, for it isn't through any excess of morals that I haven't just as many furs and pearls; it is simply because I don't see life that way, as, ten years ago, I didn't see life as the wife of an old man whom I adored but didn't love, and couldn't have thought of marrying him even if he had promised to arrange for his death an hour after the wedding. . . . Do you understand, Dikran? For all this while I've been trying to tell you that whatever else I am not, I am an honest woman; a very upright gentleman in my way, which is more than you can say for most really nice women.

'The reason why realistic tragedies are impossible, or at best only melodramatic, on the stage is that the Person who arranges life has no sense of drama at all. Imagine how Sardou, the wretched man who turned Sarah Bernhardt into an exhibition, would have worked it out: the young girl would have run away from the lustful old man to Nice; the old man would have followed her to her boarding-house and made faces at the landlady's fair-haired son, who was the girl's destiny; a duel, tears, another duel, more tears, and Sarah falling about the stage in exhausted attitudes, as well she might. . . . And then imagine how life worked out the tragedy of that girl and old man; it let them be, or it seemed to let them be! No, God can have no dramatic sense, as we know it, because all the tragedies He arranges for us are slow moving, so slow and moving none of the actors know whither; perhaps this tragedy we are acting will fade away, they say hopefully to themselves, and leave us again happy and careless; a little later they are happily sure that their tragedy is fading, there is no possible climax in sight, and then suddenly, out of the inmost earth, from some really foul spot of their animal natures, comes the sudden ingredients for the tragical climax; the climax lasts only a second, but after it no blessed curtain falls; God has interfered again, Life is more cruel than Art, He says, so away with your tricks, your curtains and your finales. And I suppose he is right, you know; it must be right that shameful memories live beside the beautiful ones, as twenty years from now the memory of that old man and myself will live beside this very moment of you and I under this willow; for my abundant confession of it all seems to make it as much yours as mine, Dikran.

'My guardian and I lived on smoothly enough, then; as before I broke out now and again when he stepped too sternly between myself and an amusing indiscretion, but rebellions always ended in my smiling at some cutting remark of his, and in his always sweet dismissal of the subject; there was nothing to show that we were different with each other. But we were, indeed we were. I did not know it then, but I knew it very clearly later; how we two people, really loving each other, though in our different ways, had found a deep, subtle antagonism in each other, a very real antagonism, which it would have shamed us to realize at the time, and with a very real and inevitable climax; but like God's creatures, mummers in yet

74

another of His cruelly monstrous plays, we thought the tragedy was fading, had faded, and were forgetting it, for what climax could there possibly be?

'Four or five months after that May morning he took me to stay at a château in Brittany; a very beautiful, tumble-down, draughty place, my dear, standing proudly at the head of a valley like a dissipated actor who feels that he must have done great things in the past to be what he now is, and with nothing to show for its draughty arrogance but a few rakish stones which were once the embattlement from which the Huguenot *seigneur* of the day defied the old Medici; and the slim, white-haired old woman who charmingly met me at the door, the châtelaine of only one castle, but with the dignity of an empire in her kind, calm elegance. My hostess and my guardian were old, old friends, and to watch them in their gentle, courteous intimacy was a lesson on the perfect management of such things. When we are old and white-haired, will you come and stay at my place, Dikran, and will you pretend that you have forgotten that you ever liked me for anything else than my mind? Just like those two old people in the Breton château, who a thousand years ago may have been lovers or may have only loved one another. . . . Who knows? and does it matter?

'The idea of this visit, on my guardian's part, to the solitary château from whose highest windows one could just see the sea curling round the Breton coast, was of course excellent. He wanted me to be out of harm's way and entirely his own, and was there any better way of achieving that than by putting me in a lonely château with only my hostess as an alternative to himself? But, poor old dear, it didn't fall out like that; for we had only been there two days when the alternative presented himself in the person of the young man of the house, my hostess' son, the young lord of Tumbledown Castle. . . . He went and spoilt it all, good and proper, did that young man. His mother hadn't expected him, my guardian didn't want him, and I didn't mind him—there he was, all the way from England on a sudden desire to see his mother, the only woman whom Raoul had ever a decent thought about, I suppose. (His name wasn't really Raoul, you know, but it is a sort of convention that all young Frenchmen with the title of Vicomte and with languid eyes and fragile natures are called Raoul.) For he wasn't by any means a nice young man, except facially, but how was I to know that! And besides, the man could sit a horse as gallantly as any young prince who ever went crusading, and I strained my eyes in prolonging the little thrill I had when, the morning after he came, I saw him from a window riding out of the gates and down into the valley, very much the young lord of the manor, on the huge white stallion which, with such a master, defied a Republic and still proclaimed him as the *Sieur du Château-Mauvrai* to the dour and morose-minded peasants of the Breton villages. . . .

'When I say that Raoul was not a nice young man, I mean that he was a very agreeable companion; but, like little Billee, in "Trilby," and Maurice, the stone image of my dreams, that poor young man couldn't love, it wasn't in him to love; but unlike the other two, who were sweet about it and made up for it as much as they could, Raoul had taken it into his head that love was all stuff and nonsense, anyway, and that he could do a deal better with the very frequent and not very fastidious pretences of it, and, according to his little-minded lights, he seems to have been right, for he had already done fairly well for himself in London—this I found much later, of course—with a flat in Mayfair which was much more consistent with the various middle-aged ladies who came to tea with him than with the extent of his income.

'No reasonable person could expect that a young man like that and I could stay in the same house and no trouble come of it. But my guardian wasn't reasonable. He seemed still to expect me to go riding with him, and let a perfectly good young man run to waste for want of a companion to say pretty things to. Raoul and I, in that beautiful spot, were scarcely ever allowed to be alone, and only twice did we manage to ride away together to the sea for a delicious, exciting few hours; only twice, I said, for the second time was very definitely the last. . . . Somehow the Marquis was always there. Not in any unpleasant way, but he would just happen to come into the room or the particular corner of the large garden where we also happened to be; he didn't rebuke or look sulky, he was just the same, except, perhaps, for a little irony to Raoul, whom he refused to take seriously as a young man of the world. And that is where the old man made his mistake with me, for I, too, didn't take Raoul seriously; I took him for just what he was, more knave than fool, a charming companion, and a very personable young man, as far as being just "personable" counts, and only so far. If I had been allowed to deal with the matter in my own way, without let or hindrance, it would only have been very pleasant trifling, and certainly no more; even as it was, the "no more" part of it was still safe in my keeping, thanks entirely to my having brought myself up properly; but for the rest a simple amusement became a rather sordid tragedy, for God and guardian had combined to use a commonplace young man as the climax to a faded and forgotten little fantasy, once sun-kissed by a May morning, now to be shivered and scattered by the shrieking sea wind, discordant chorus enough for the unmingled destinies of any Tristans and Isoldas, which kept forcing our horses apart on that last morning of all, when we three rode by the sea, and made a world of anger for ourselves because someone, something, had suddenly pushed us out of the other world where we had been so careless and happy. . . .

'Once things happened, they happened quickly. For all my not taking him at all seriously, I suppose I liked him quite a lot, really—I must have done, else I would not have been such a fool. He was my first experience of dishonesty in man, and I suppose I wanted to plumb this dishonesty of his to the depths, which was very stupid of me because he was much more likely to find out about me than I about him. . . . Raoul had been at the château two weeks and our little affair had taken the important and unpleasant air of a conspiracy. Our own stay was to last another month, and if it hadn't been that my guardian would not for the world have offended his old friend by cutting short this long-looked-for visit, he would very soon have taken me away from the so desecrating gaze of young Raoul.

77

'On that day, towards evening, he and I had managed to steal out walking for an hour. Agreeable enough as he was, he would have bored me if I had let him. But I wanted him, I intended to keep him in my mind, I wanted him as an assertion of my independence from the old man. As we went back up the drive to the château I carefully became as animated and smiling as I could, for I knew that he would be watching us from the drawing-room windows, and I wanted to irritate him as much as his incessant care was irritating me, though that would have been impossible, for that evening I was absurdly, fiercely angry with him. Life seemed made up of the interferences of old men. I didn't want old men in my life. I wanted young men, and sunshine, and fun. And so, as Raoul and I went up the steps to the massive door, and as I turned to him just below the drawing-room window and gave him my most trustful smile, I was feeling reckless, unrestrained, fiercely independent. . . . Oh, Dikran! what idiocies we do for the fancied sake of independence!

'It was time to dress for dinner, so I left Raoul and went straight to my room. A minute later came a knock on the door, and as I turned sharply from the mirror, it opened and Raoul stood there, rather shy, smiling. I wasn't old enough to know the proper way of dealing with young men in one's bedroom, even if I had overpoweringly wanted to.

' "I had an impulse," he said, but he still stood in the doorway, a little question somewhere about him. I didn't answer it; just watched him, rather interested in his methods.

' "Because," he went on, "I used to sleep in this room once, and remember it as a dreary little place, and I wanted to see what it looked like with you in it." Poor silly fool, I thought, but rather loved him. I have found since then, though, that his fatuous speech was quite the proper one to make, for the established way of entering a woman's room is by expressing an interest in the furniture, thus making the lady self-conscious and not so sure about her dignity; seductions are successful through women fearing to look fools if they refuse to be seduced.

'But this time, as he spoke, he closed the door behind

him and came into the room towards me. "This isn't playing fair, Raoul," I only said; "you will get me into a row."

' "Fair!" he said, lifting his eyebrows, the gallant ass. "My sweet, do you think anything real is fair in this world? And don't you trust me? That isn't fair of you, you know—haven't I made love to you for two weeks, haven't I loved you for two weeks, haven't I loved you all my life—and now?" And with that he had me in his arms, not for the first time, mind you, but this time very differently; and, over his shoulder, as he held me, I saw the door open, and the Marquis stood there, outraged. Raoul didn't seem to know, still held me, and I, for a paralysed moment, couldn't move, just stared at the old man standing very stiffly in the doorway, a hand outstretched on the door knob—hell seemed to have opened for him through that door, and he could move as little as I. At last I jumped away from Raoul with a sort of cry, and he turned quickly round to the door. He didn't go pale, or look a fool; he must have made a study of such contretemps; nothing was said, the old man waiting in the doorway, with words terribly smothered; he moved aside a little from the door as though to let a dog slink through. But Raoul wasn't going to slink; he was rather pink, negligent, resigned; and as, without the least hurry, he bent over my fingers and his eyes smiled gently at me, I found myself admiring him, really loving him for the first time. Women are like that. . . . All this, of course, had happened in less than a minute from point of time my guardian came into my room and Raoul left it—but in point of fact a great deal happened. For, as Raoul left me and walked across the room to the door, and through it without taking the least notice of the old man, and as I heard his even steps receding down the parquet corridor, my first paralysed fear simmered in me and boiled up into a fierce, vixen anger. I simply trembled now with anger at the old man as I had first trembled with fear of him. What right had he to be standing there, ordering about my life and my young men? What right had he to be closing the door, as he was doing now? What right, what right? The words were throbbing inside me, just those words, fixed unrestrainedly on the old man, who had made a step towards me, and stopped again. . . .

' "Child!" the pain in that one word, the lack of anger in it, an utter, absolute pain accusing me, did not soothe. Accuse me? By what right?

'That scene was dreadful, Dikran. I can't tell you what we said, what I said, for I did most of the scene-making. He just forbade me to talk again alone with Raoul or to go out with him; said he would take me away tomorrow if it weren't that explanations would then be necessary to our hostess, who was in feeble health and might be killed by such a disgrace as this in her own house. As for Monsieur le Vicomte, he himself would arrange that I did not see him for longer time than could be helped. That's all he said, but my white heat took little notice of his commands. I said I don't know what—but it must all have been terrible, for it ended on a terrible note. Dikran, how could I have done it? I pointed at the door and asked him how he could think he had more right in my room than Raoul, for though he was my guardian our relations had been changed by a certain proposal, which perhaps he remembered. . . . A look at me, in which was the first and last contempt that's ever been given me, and the door closed on the wonderful old man.

'Dinner that night passed off quite well considering the unsettled climatic conditions aforesaid. Myself didn't contribute much, but my guardian and Raoul talked smoothly away about anything that came, while Madame, our hostess, smiled sweetly at us all, on brooding me in particular. . . . Quite early I made for bed; the old man and I hadn't exchanged a word all evening, and his "good night" was a little bow, and mine cold. As I passed Raoul he cleverly put a small piece of paper into my hand. Upstairs in my room, that piece of paper said that he would be going away in a day or two, and would I ride with him tomorrow morning before breakfast, at seven o'clock. Of course I would.

'It was all a silly business, Dikran. If I had even been in love with Raoul, I certainly wasn't that morning when we rode away from the gloomy, silent château, a little frightened by our own bravado; for that is all it was. But later, as we reached the sands, I forgot that, I forgot Raoul, though of course he always talked; I was enjoying the horse under me, the summer morning, the high sea wind dashing its salt air against my cheeks; I was enjoying every one of those things more than the company of the young man, but, tragically, my guardian could not know that.

'We had been out about half an hour when Raoul, looking back over his shoulder, murmured, "Ah!" "What is it!" I asked. I could barely force my little voice through the wind. "That old man," Raoul said indifferently. "It seems that he too is out to take the salt air." Yes, there was a figure on horse-back, perhaps half a mile behind us but rapidly gaining on our slow canter. I had forgotten my anger, but now again it thrust itself viciously on me.

' "Come on, let's give him a run," I said, a little excitedly.

' "Oh, no! I am not a baby to be chased about by my own guests or other people's grandfathers!"

'Affected idiot, I thought, and we rode on in silence. So really silly it all was, my dear; for if it hadn't been for my anger, the natural reaction, in a way, of the muffled life I had led with him, I had much sooner been riding with the old man than with the young one. But that feeling didn't last long—no one gave it a chance to last. For at last, after what seemed an age, his horse drew beside mine, and I heard his voice distantly through the wind, saying, "Sandra! You must come back." I didn't answer, but worse, I looked sideways at him and laughed. It was the first time that I had ever seen him in the least bit ridiculous, and my laugh took advantage of it. Raoul was a yard or so ahead of us and was giving his horse rein, and so I put mine to the gallop—and heigh-ho! there were the three of us racing away on the Breton sands—until, with wonderful and dangerous horsemanship, my guardian's horse leapt a yard or so ahead and swung broadside round in front of our startled horses. Near as anything there were three broken collar-bones. Our horses reared high up, almost fell backwards, nearly braining the old man with their frantic hoofs, and then at last took the ground, startled and panting. My guardian didn't wait. He pointed his whip at Raoul and said sternly, "If I were not a guest at your mother's house I would thrash you, for that is what you need"; and then to me, harshly, "Come, Sandra. Enough of this nonsense. Home."

' "Not I," I cried against the wind. "I'm enjoying my ride." And round his horse I went, towards the sea, leaving them to their argument. I almost wanted him to follow me, I was so bitterly angry. I don't know what I thought I would do—but I suppose I didn't think.

'I must have galloped two hundred yards or so when he was beside me again. I took no notice; we rode on, almost knee to knee. And then I saw his hand stretch out, clutch my rein, and pull; I saw red, I saw nothing, or just his old, lined face bending over . . . and, my dear. I swung my riding-whip as hard as I could across it. The hand left my rein, but my horse had already been pulled up. I don't remember what happened. I stared at him as unbelievingly as he stared at me. I seemed to see a weal across his face where my whip had struck him—had I done that? And then he smiled, Dikran, that dear old man smiled after that horrible insult, so sweetly and sadly.

' "That then is the end, my child," he said very gently; and then he left me, and for a long time I watched him as he rode slowly away. Frightfully ashamed. . . .

'It was done, irretrievably; such things can't be forgiven, except in words; and as far as words went he, of course, forgave me. A few hours later I saw him in the hall; he was going to pass me, but suddenly I flung my arms about him, begging him . . . very pitiful, dreadful thing I was. He was splendid. He said very softly into my ear that of course he forgave me, but that he was too old to have a proper control over his memory, and so couldn't forget, and that he was too old to be hurt any more, and so this would be the very last time, for he didn't think it would be wise for me to live with him any more. "Sandra, my child, you must not think me too unkind for sending you away, but I think it is the best plan. You have lived with an old man long enough—it was a mistake. I see now that it was a mistake. You must forgive me, child. I was wrong to keep you so long. I thought, perhaps, it might have been different. . . ." He was inexorable about that, and it wasn't

82

my place to, I couldn't beg him to keep me. I, who had hurt him so much!

'He must have made some excuse to our hostess, for the next day saw us in Paris. Raoul? Oh, I never noticed him any more. And two days later I was with a stodgy uncle in Portman Square, hating London but hating myself more. I have been miserable many times, but never so shamefacedly as then, during the two weeks which passed between my arrival in London and the coming of that note from the old man's valet, saying that Monsieur le Marquis was very ill, and the doctor said he would die; and so he had taken the liberty of writing to me, without permission, in case I should like to go and see him; would I be so kind as not to tell Monsieur le Marquis that he had written to me?

'Like a young woman to a dying lover, I went to Paris, and with a terrible flutter in my heart stood on the doorstep of the stern-looking house in the *Rue Colbert*. . . . They hadn't told him I was coming, but he must have expected me, for there was no surprise in the smile with which he met the timid little figure which came into his room. He seemed to me not ill, but just dying; he looked the same, only very tired. And then I realized that he was dying because he wanted to die. An angry girl had shown him that life was indeed not worth living, and so he was stopping his heart with his own hand. . . . It was terrible to realize that as I stood by his bed and he smiled quite gaily up at me. The weakness was too strong inside him, and he couldn't speak, just patted my hand and held it very tightly. . . . I was very glad when I was out of that room, and I did not see him again before he died early the next morning.

'And so you see, Dikran, for all your talk of *dies iræ* in the future, I've already had my *dies iræ*, and very sadly, too—and been the wiser for it in restraint.'

*　　　*　　　*

Then it was that I realized with a start that my housemaid was staring at me from the door in the grey March morning, and that I was not listening to Shelmerdene in a backwater of the Thames, but was in London, where there is less time for cherishing one's own ideals than for enquiring into other people's. . . .